Black Smokers

By
CJ Waller

Damnation Books, LLC.
P.O. Box 3931
Santa Rosa, CA 95402-9998
www.damnationbooks.com

Black Smokers
by CJ Waller

Digital ISBN: 978-1-62929-059-1
Print ISBN: 978-1-62929-060-7

Cover art by: Dawné Dominique
Edited by: Andrea Heacock-Reyes

Printed in the United States of America
Worldwide Electronic & Digital Rights
Worldwide English Language Print Rights

I'd like to dedicate this book to my daughters, Lucy and Emily. Their boundless curiosity is a constant reminder of how wonderful and strange the world is.

I would like to thank each and every member of The Word Cloud (but especially Wrathnar the Unreasonable)—I wouldn't be where I am today without all your help and advice. Also, Dave Rozzell... you are a star. Finally, HP Lovecraft, whose writings inspired me to explore my weird side and write about the things I love, no matter how mad they may be.

In 1997, the U.S. National Oceanic and Atmospheric Administration (NOAA) recorded an ultra-low frequency sound in the Pacific Ocean, off the coast of South America. They called it "the Bloop". It was inconsistent with anything man-made, such as submarines or explosives, or anything geological such as earthquakes or volcanic activity. Initially, it was suggested it might have been the result of an iceberg breaking up in Antarctica. A year later, NOAA updated this to suggest the Bloop was probably animal in origin. The problem with this hypothesis is that the sound was picked up 4800 kilometers apart, meaning it was far louder and stronger than any marine animal alive today is capable of making.

Since then, the Bloop has been attributed back to icequakes.

Others do not necessarily believe this.

Chapter One

"Ten thousand four hundred and sixty-three feet..."

For once, we were silent. No bickering, no jokes. Nothing. Just the faint whine of the electric engine and the occasional splutter of bubbles rising from the re-breather to the distant surface above us broke the peace.

We hovered for a moment, motionless above the endless sands. The world beyond our reinforced Perspex world was black and cold. I pushed the little joystick controlling the sub forward, and its propellers kicked up the sediment. It reduced visibility, already low, to nothing.

Out of the murk, a sheer cliff loomed. Ailsa screamed, and it reverberated around us. Brett stuffed his fingers into his ears, but I had no such luxury. I wrenched the stick back, and the sub pitched upward until its momentum slowed. Quiet reigned once again.

"You fucking idiot!" Brett seethed, running trembling hands through messy locks. "We nearly hit that outcrop!"

I hardly heard him, and even if I had, I wouldn't have cared. My heart still thundered in my ears, blocking out all other sounds. Where the hell had that come from?

Having had no joy with me, Brett focused his ire on Ailsa.

"Weren't you supposed to monitor for things like this? What is wrong with you?"

"Don't blame me," Ailsa spat back. "There was nothing to indicate an outcrop out there!" She shot me an evil look as she leaned over to peer at one of the tiny screens, tracing the glowing figures with one finger.

"See? Nothing on the SONAR." A flicker of fear rippled across her face. "It's like it literally appeared out of nowhere."

As one, we turned our attention from the monitor to the tiny window ahead of us. The sub had drifted a little in unseen currents, turning us about.

"It looks volcanic," Ailsa said, her geologist's sensibilities overcoming her fright. "That would make sense, given the sudden shift in the sea bed." She frowned. "Still doesn't explain why the instruments didn't pick it up, though."

"Maybe, you weren't reading them right," Brett said, still visibly shaken.

"Maybe, you just need to shut up," Ailsa said.

"Maybe, you could both leave this until later," I said. "We've only got another hour down here tops. I don't know about you, but I don't want to spend it arguing."

Both Ailsa and Brett shot me a venomous look, like sulky teenagers forced into obeying their father. It worried me that we were arguing at all. Usually, we all got along pretty well, but something has happened to us all down here. I couldn't put my finger on it, but more than the atmospheric pressure was rising.

We followed the outcrop for a good hundred feet until it dropped back beneath the sediment. Beyond its sheer walls, massive clouds of what looked like black smoke belched from cracks in the earth's surface. I felt my heart quicken, this time with excitement. Just as we had hoped, the recent seismic shifts had created new vents, and even from our position, we could all see fledgling colonies of huge, polychaete tubeworms snaking their way around the base of the smokers, their red plumage waving in the superheated water.

No...that couldn't be right. Doubt raised its unwelcome head, and my elation dropped a notch. It usually took over a century for a deep-water tubeworm to grow a few feet. Yet, these monsters managed at least six feet in three short weeks. I dared to nudge the stick forward, bringing *The Aurora* a little closer to the vents. The worms twisted their crimson bodies toward us, their pink-tinged tentacles bidding us welcome.

"What are they doing?" Brett asked. "It's like they know we're here."

"Impossible," Ailsa said. "I might not be the biology expert, but even *I* know worms are worms, wherever they are found."

I held my breath, mesmerized. Tiny crustaceans that looked like a mixture of crab and shrimp scuttled around the worms' rocky bases, and I thought I spied a fish no bigger than my thumb fleeing from our lights with a flick of its tiny tail. From out of the depths, something large darted forward and grasped one of the exposed worms, pulling it from its calcareous tube.

"What the—" Ailsa gasped as the creature sped off again into the darkness. "Did you guys just see that?"

My surprise rendered me dumb, and all I could do was nod.

"It couldn't have been..." Brett said. "I mean, they've been extinct for, uh—"

"About 530,000,000 years," I said. Even to me, my voice sounded hoarse. "Or around that mark."

The creature swam forward again, fragments of the worm still caught in its mandible-like jaws.

"*Anomalacaris...*" Ailsa whispered. "Burgess Shale fauna, British Columbia." Her eyes were like saucers as she watched the bizarre animal. It seized another polychaete, plucking it from its tube with ease. "But none of them were this *big...*"

She trailed off and joined the rest of us in awed silence. Its meal finished, the ancient arthropod turned gracefully upon one lobed, wing-like fin and sped off into the abyssal night.

"Quick, follow it!" Brett lunged at the sticks and grabbed them from my hands. The sub lurched forward, its engine screaming. The *Anomalacaris*, startled by our pursuit, fled.

"Are you insane?" I wrestled him away from the controls. "We're right on the edge, Brett. This sub hasn't been tested for manned expeditions below 10,500 feet!" I glanced toward the fuel gauge. "Plus, we have less than an hour's worth of juice left before we have to resurface—gunning after *anything* severely reduces our time down here."

"What?" Brett's incredulity was palpable. "We've just seen a creature that was supposed to have died out over 500 million years ago...and you don't want to know more?" He threw his hands up, narrowly missing Ailsa. "That was the find of a lifetime, Tom, and you've just let it slip through our fingers—"

"It's not a find if we get stranded," I said. "Need I remind you that there will be no rescue service down here—"

"So much for your intrepid sense of adventure! I can't believe you, sometimes. I really ca—"

"Shut up," Ailsa said, her eyes glued to the monitor in front of her.

"What?" Brett rounded upon her. Even I felt my hackles rise a little.

"I said shut up." She stabbed the screen with her finger. "There's something out there. It's only just appeared. Some kind of...construction. I don't know, but it's too regular to be natural...and it's big." She looked up at us both, excitement chasing concern.

"Could just be another outcrop," I said. "Some kind of basalt intrusion?"

Brett, his argument with me forgotten, peered over Ailsa's shoulder.

"No, Tom...look at it. It's perfectly square." He whistled. "And huge..."

The SONAR readout pulsed again, clearly showing a huge cube. It was surrounded by smaller readings which seemed to wink in and out of existence.

"What are those things around it?" Brett asked.

"I'm not sure," Ailsa replied. "Tom?"

I scrutinized the screen for a long while, caressing my top lip with my index finger.

"I don't know," I said, defeated. "I guess we'll have to go and have a look."

Brett shot me a triumphant look.

"Now, we're talking!"

Ailsa looked up at the pair of us, worry tugging at her brow.

"Guys—maybe we should do this later? Go back up, recharge the batteries, and study the footage we already have?"

Her suggestion was as reasonable as it was sensible. I knew that, but it was too late. I seized the controls and pushed them forward, urging the sub through the field of smokers, toward the anomalous cube.

"Guys..."

"We're just going to look," Brett said. "What does the monitor say?"

Ailsa sighed and focused back on the screens. A tense silence settled back over us as we powered onward.

"Wait a sec...this is really weird." Ailsa looked up from the SONAR and switched her attention to the thermal imaging monitor. She flicked the screen with her finger. I gestured for Brett to take the controls, so I could take a look.

She wasn't wrong.

"What the hell is going on?" I murmured, more to myself than anyone else.

"I know," Ailsa said. "They seem to form a path. There's no other way to describe it."

I glanced out of the window. Beads of condensation ran down the pane. They pooled in the bottom lip and dripped onto my knee. I watched as the drips spread and merged together, finding each other through the wiry forest of my leg hair before running down my calf. I shivered. For some reason, I was reminded of the magma that seethed just beneath the sea bed. *Before they pool together and pour forth...*

I shook my head to clear the image and focused again upon the smokers that bubbled on either side of us. According to the thermal imager, they were far from random in their placement. The cracks from which they boiled formed two parallel lines leading directly to the cube.

As Ailsa said, like a path.

A little, red warning light began to blink.

"We're at 10,500 feet," Ailsa murmured. We shared a look and turned as one to Brett. His attention fixed firmly on the little spot of light our sub produced, he showed no outward sign that he had heard her. Ailsa offered me an anxious look. I simply shrugged back. I had no clue what was wrong with him, either.

The little, red light continued to blink. Something in my chest tightened a notch. The *Aurora* was designed to reach depths of 12,000 feet, but it had only been tested to 10,500. We had thought that more than adequate—hell, why test deeper when the sea floor was only supposed to be 8,000 feet away? Now, even with prior echo-sounding data that informed us of the 2,000-foot drop three weeks previously, we thought the sub's capabilities well within our demands.

Ten thousand five hundred and sixty-two feet.

A low creak joined the engines. I swallowed hard to clear my ears as the pressure mounted. Ailsa, her pulse fluttering visibly in her throat, leaned forward to place a shaking hand on Brett's shoulder.

"Uh, Brett? Maybe, it's time to give up and head to shallower waters. You know the sub hasn't actively been tested at this depth, and well, I don't think we shoul—"

The sub juddered and pitched to one side, throwing Ailsa into my arms. I caught her awkwardly, my vision temporarily obscured by a veil of blonde hair. The *Aurora* groaned again, its metal protesting at this blatant abuse. The red light, like a baleful eye, kept blinking.

Ten thousand six hundred and twenty-four feet.

"Brett!" I demanded as I untangled myself from Ailsa's flailing limbs. "Stop this!" I stumbled forward and clapped my hand upon his shoulder with the intention of wrenching him out of the seat, but his neck was like iron. I glanced again at his reflection in the glass and knew by the maniacal gleam in his eyes that he was lost to us.

"Can you hear them?" he whispered. "Can you? They're in there—the trapped, the lost. He called them all those years ago in preparation for this day, and now, the time is finally right. Just a few more feet, and you'll see..."

Another surge buffeted the sub, sending me sprawling backward. One after the other, the monitors fizzled out, their screens dissolving into static. Still, Brett forced the *Aurora* forward, following that tiny spot of light along the sea floor. Things scurried out of our path upon jointed legs, snapping their oversized claws at us as we passed. The black smokers now reached unprecedented size, towering over us on each side, their accompanying tubeworms creating huge forests of calcareous tubes while their tentacled heads leered down upon us.

I reached behind myself and fumbled at the straps of a spare oxygen tank. Ailsa, her eyes wide, sat upon the floor in stupid terror and watched dumbly as Brett—passionate, brilliant Brett—continued to mutter to himself, gibbering on and on about the stars and how they were finally right, and that now...maybe, after all these years, they would finally let her go—

I felt the strap loosen. I pulled it open and wrapped my fingers securely around the neck of the tank. Just one, hard smack should do it. Not to kill, of course—just incapacitate. Then, up and out of this alien world. I suppose I should have realized there was no way Brett would cope with such a discovery. As brilliant as he was, his constant chatter about ancient gods sleeping under the ocean should have alerted me to his mental state. I was so keen—too *desperate*—to succeed that I ignored the signs, made excuses, dismissed his talk as over-imaginative nonsense, and concentrated upon his remarkable affinity for marine sciences.

The canister was heavier than I remembered. I lifted it clumsily and raised it over my head, preparing myself for what I had to do.

Everything went dark.

I dropped the canister with a clang that echoed throughout the sub. Ailsa, her fright too much to scream, whimpered.

"Do you see?" Brett whispered. "Out there...do you see?"

My throat threatened to close up as the sub filled with an

eerie, green light. Brett, silhouetted by its brilliance, stood up, still clutching the controls. Ahead of us, a rolling vista unfolded. I forgot my alarm at Brett's behavior and watched, awestruck, as vast arcs of what resembled green electricity leaped from the pinnacles of towering pillars carved out of a shining, black rock. They formed a rough circle, and the cube sat at the center, squat and ugly.

Out of the gloom, something huge swam past us. It had to be forty feet in length, and there was something hideously prehistoric about its form. It didn't seem to notice our presence as it buffeted the sub, which sent us spinning toward the stone circle. This time, Ailsa *did* scream, and for a moment, I wondered if she would ever stop. I braced myself against the bulkhead, my heart hammering inside my ribcage while the *Aurora* creaked and groaned around me. One of the monitors—I don't know which one—shattered, peppering us with tiny fragments of glass. Brett, his attention still firmly fixed on the plain below, began to laugh—a low cackle that made the hairs upon the nape of my neck rise.

"They know we're here," he said. He turned to me, his eyes wild. "There's no escape, now. None."

"Shut up! Shut up!" Ailsa screamed and lunged for him, only to be thrown aside as the sub spun around, again. As the pillars loomed closer, part of me felt oddly detached. They weren't constructed from one piece of stone, but out of many interlocking pieces. I was aware of a scuffle behind me, but it was nothing more than an irritation as I studied those stones. I cocked my head to one side, trying to fit the pieces together in my head, but what I could see stubbornly refused to fit. A pain deep within my head flared, forcing me to look away.

The sound came from nowhere. It began as a low hum that reverberated throughout the *Aurora*. There was a plink as another screen gave way. The hum rose to a cacophonous roar, forcing Ailsa and Brett to quit their arguing and clap their hands over their ears. Ailsa dropped to the floor, her eyes screwed shut. Brett, on the other hand, looked strangely exultant. He raised his arms in apparent ecstasy and began to shout, his words drowned out by the hum. It rose again, and strange harmonies now joined it. My vision began to waver. I staggered backward, tears streaming down my face, and I slumped against the wall.

I don't remember anything else.

Chapter Two

29th February, Sixteen Years Earlier

"I can't believe you're doing this to me. This place *stinks*!" Marissa kicked a stone. It skittered across the dusty road and struck the ageing wood of the wharf with a dull thud.

"Marissa, shut up." Mom sighed, her lips drawn in a tight line. "I've had just enough of your whining. You don't see Brett going on so!"

Brett allowed himself a smug smile.

"It's not Brett's birthday!" Marissa continued petulantly. "I wanted to go somewhere special on my birthda—"

"*Marissa!*" Even Brett knew not to push it when Mom took on that tone of voice. "Your father wanted to share this holiday with you, and you're going to damn well pretend you're enjoying it. Do I make myself clear?"

Brett watched the conflict crawl across his sister's face, and for a moment, he thought that her argumentative side would win. Thankfully, she just nodded, her mouth screwed up in an ugly pout.

"Look what I've got!" A voice floated across the oily waters of the quay, full of unbridled glee. "Ice cream!"

Marissa rolled her eyes and folded her arms tightly over her budding chest. Brett fought down the urge to punch her and made sure he was smiling as their father approached, four dripping cones in his hands.

"One for Brett...one for Mom...and one for the Birthday Girl!" He beamed, holding out the treat as if it was the Olympic Torch. Marissa, stubborn as ever, did not accept her prize. Brett's heart sank a little as the smile on his father's face faltered.

"What's up, honey?"

"Nothing, Daddy," Marissa replied. Brett knew the reversion to baby-talk was a deliberate ploy. She took the ice cream cone. "Thank you."

Dad grinned again and leaned against the weather-stained rail that surrounded the wharf. Above them, seagulls wheeled and complained. Beneath them, the sea lapped lazily against ancient pilings, groaning under the weight of massive growths of mussels and barnacles.

The breeze picked up, ruffling Brett's hair. He wrinkled his nose as he ate his cone. No matter how much of a brat Marissa was being, she was right. This place did smell. Old fish, rotten seaweed, and something else...something he couldn't quite put his finger on, but it made his eyes water nonetheless.

In the distance, a few old fishermen sat mending nets, their sullen eyes watching the family as they meandered along the shoreline. Dad had been really excited about coming back here. His great grandfather was from Innsmouth, and it had a colorful past—adventures on the South Seas and pacts with ancient gods, smugglers, and pirates. As a small boy, those tales enthralled Brett, and he begged his father to tell him more, more, more! Dad just smiled a little sadly and shook his head. "One day, I'll take you there," he replied and then left Brett to dream of the vast deeps and the sea monsters that dwelt there.

Well, they were now here. It wasn't entirely as Brett had imagined. In his mind's eye, he had populated Innsmouth with bawdy pirates, and later on, in the throes of his burgeoning adolescence, buxom wenches. His imaginary wharf was a bustling place, filled with schooners and galleons, their sails fluttering in the wind while the sailors wound their way along crooked, narrow streets, looking for dark taverns to drink in. The reality was far less impressive. Yes, there were sailors, but they consisted of odd-looking fishermen who eyed them suspiciously as they walked along the dockside. The streets were indeed narrow and crooked, but there were no taverns— just neglected houses with flaking paint and boards instead of windows. Even the boats were wrong. There were no galleons. Instead, squat fishing boats that belched out clouds of greasy smoke tugged up to their moorings, their nets filled with ugly, misshapen fish and a proliferation of squid.

One such boat chugged past them, the smoke from its exhaust making Brett's mother cough. Marissa, her face a picture of disgust, waved a flamboyant hand in front of her nose. The seagulls screamed as one of the fishermen leapt from the vessel's gunwale and ran alongside it, a grubby length of rope in his hands. To Brett, his gait seemed awkward. He hopped more than ran as he tried to keep up until the skipper threw the boat back into reverse. Finally, it stopped, and the skipper scuttled from the cabin to the back of the trawler. A laden net swung over the jetty, the bottom of which then released, and a torrent of fish spewed forth and filled the filthy, plastic box his mate had placed to gather the catch.

A fish leapt in a bid for freedom. It flopped onto the quayside and lay there, gasping for breath. Brett felt something inside him flip. The fish was unlike anything he had ever seen, with a long, sinuous body that flared into a flat, bulbous head that housed a pair of massive jaws. In those jaws nestled row upon row of sharp, needle-like teeth, which it snapped together. Its eyes weren't much more than pinpricks, but they sought out Brett's nonetheless. With a croak, the fisherman drew a crude cudgel from his belt and brought it down sharply upon the fish's slime-covered head. It spasmed violently at the impact, and there was a crack as its skull gave way. Viscous grey matter splattered up, coating the fisherman. Some of it landed on the concrete floor in front of Brett.

A hand descended upon his shoulder, causing his heart to jump painfully in his chest.

"Come on, buddy," Dad murmured. "I don't think there's any point in hanging around here."

Brett swallowed down the lump of bile that had collected in his throat and nodded. He took his father's hand and allowed himself to be led away like a small child. He risked a glance back, and the men were unloading a second net into another box, clubbing any escapees between them and returning them to the catch. They grunted to each other as they did so, and one even paused to light a cigarette. That bothered Brett the most. Not their actions, but their complete indifference to the lives they were extinguishing with each casual thud of their cudgels.

The wind picked up even more, bringing with it a thin veil of drizzle. In the distance, thunder rumbled. The fishermen paused from their gruesome work to gaze over the ocean. Other people joined them from the derelict buildings, and between them, they hoisted the plastic boxes holding the catch of the day onto their shoulders and whisked them away. A few stragglers glared at them. Brett's father squeezed his hand.

"Better get back to the car," he said.

"What's wrong with those people, Dad?" Brett asked.

His father paused for a moment.

"They don't get many visitors. So, we're a bit of a novelty."

"That's not what I meant...they walk weird. They *look* weird."

"That's not a nice thing to say, Brett," said his father.

"But it's true!" Brett said. "Look at them."

"Well...this is a working community. People have accidents, I guess—"

Brett's dad stopped and turned to the sea, a confused look upon his face. A low rumble, more felt than heard, rolled in over the waves and carried with it weird harmonics that made Brett's ears ache. It continued to rise to a bellowing crescendo—an ear-splitting cacophony of clicks, screams, and a deep, booming roar that forced Brett to screw his eyes up tightly and cover his ears with his hands. He felt something warm and sticky trickle from his nose—blood. The sound rose until Brett thought his eyes were going to rattle out of their sockets. Then, without any warning, it simply stopped.

Brett wiped his nose on his sleeve, leaving a long, red streak.

"Are you all right, son?" his dad asked. Brett could see a bubble of blood playing peek-a-boo with one of his father's nostrils. He nodded, still feeling a little shaky.

"Marissa?" His mother's voice held a note of panic.

Brett looked over at her. Why was Marissa being such a pain in the ass, today?

"Marissa?" his Mom called again, turning on the spot.

Underneath the wharf, the oily surface of the water churned. Brett watched a bubble pop, releasing a tiny package of foul gas.

"Marissa!" Brett's father joined his mother, cupping his hands around his mouth. "*Marissa!*"

Marissa was nowhere to be seen.

Chapter Three

Black swirled with gray, dancing shadows upon the edge of my consciousness. For a moment, I had no idea where I was. The stench of brine and sulfur made my nose itch, and my lungs burned with the effort of breathing the thin air. I tried to sit up. Little flowers of exquisite agony burst behind my eyes. I clutched my head and let out a low groan.

At my feet, Ailsa lay face down, her hair forming a golden corona around her head. A surge of panic cleared the pain in my head in an instant. I grasped her by the shoulders, all the rules about moving injured people forgotten. I just wanted to know if she was alive. To my utter relief, she moaned as I rolled her over. Thick, red blood trickled down the side of her face from a nasty cut to her temple.

"Ailsa? Are you okay? Can you hear me?" The question was stupid, but it was all I could think to ask. She raised a shaking hand to her head and moaned, again.

"Christ, my head...what the hell happened?" She looked up at me, her perfectly blue eyes pleading.

"I don't know. Something hit us. Then, there was that noise—"

"I remember the noise. I thought my head was going to explode." She glanced around the sub. "Hey, where's Brett?"

The note of alarm in her voice made me look up. The entrance hatchway to the sub stood open.

"What the *fuck*?"

I jumped to my feet. Pain lanced down my right leg, but I ignored it as I stretched up to close the hatch. It fell with a clang. In a fit of desperation, I deadlocked the lever that acted as the door handle.

"It's a bit late, now," Ailsa said. "Who knows how long it's been open?"

I shook my head, clutched it in my hands, and desperately tried to sort through a jumble of broken memories. Ailsa gingerly stood up and padded over to the front of the sub. Glass crunched under her feet, and every instrument was broken.

She picked over what was left of the controls and peered out of the front portal. Thin cracks spider-webbed their way across its surface. I sat and watched her, despair settling heavily upon my shoulders. After a long pause, she picked her way to the back of the sub again, strapped a headlamp on, and hoisted one of the air tanks onto her back.

"What are you doing?" I asked.

"Sitting in here isn't going to get us anywhere, Tom." She pushed the mouthpiece between her lips and took an experimental pull of air. "One way or another, we need to find out what is going on." She buckled the straps that held the tank to her back and gave me a resolute look. "Find out where we are and what's happened to Brett."

I should have known. Of course, she'd want to find Brett. Ten years younger than me, and far more the enticing prospect, despite his apparent descent into lunacy. I forced myself to hold in a burst of laughter. Here we were, God knows where, and I was worrying like a teenager about which one of us Ailsa liked best. *Time to get a grip, old man.*

I knew nothing I could say would change her mind. I'd seen that look before, and I knew better than to argue with her. I reached for my own headlamp and canister, my nervous fingers making a mockery of the tangled straps. She picked up a large, industrial-sized spanner and stuck it through her belt like a sword. I found a compass and picked up the next largest piece of kit from the emergency toolbox—a screwdriver. It paled onto insignificance next to the spanner, and I considered asking her to swap, but from the rigid set of her jaw, I guessed she wouldn't. Finally ready, I gave her a nod. A ghost of a grateful smile touched her lips. Together, we readied our mouthpieces, and I stretched up to release the door once more. She made to go up, but I ducked in front of her. She might get the spanner, but I don't think my masculinity could take her going first as well.

I scrambled up the ladder, my palms slicked with sweat, and pulled myself from the sub. All around us, mist tinged with a blue-green glow swirled. I braced myself, took a flying leap from the side of the sub, and landed with a squelch in what I initially thought was mud. The stench of brine and sulfur grew stronger, and I realized that I stood ankle-deep in some kind of algal mat. Where I landed, a thick pus-like fluid oozed, and my stomach heaved at the sight. Unable to take a deep enough breath to steady my stomach, I shoved in my mouthpiece and took a good pull of the flat-tasting air.

"Tom? Are you all right?" The querulous edge to Ailsa's voice betrayed her nervousness. She might act all brave, but I knew that inside, she was as afraid as I was. For some reason, I found that thought oddly comforting.

"Yeah," I replied. "I think so. We seem to be in some kind of…some kind of cavern. I think. It's slippery out here. So, be careful."

Ailsa clung to the top of the sub and allowed herself to slide down its side rather than jump as I had done. She landed with a short scream and disappeared. I lunged forward, not caring that I now wallowed in the putrid algae, and scrabbled in the muck for her flailing hands. I grasped her wrists and pulled as hard as I could. Her nails dug into my slime-covered skin, and her breath came in ragged gasps as she heaved herself from the concealed pool. Only then did I realize how cold the water was, and that Ailsa was freezing.

"C-c-c-cold!" she stuttered through bluing lips. Lacking any other options, I wrapped my arms around her and tried to ignore the way her body fit against mine.

The cold that infused her was so strong that it stole the heat from my body, and it wasn't long before I was shivering, too. Still, I held her tightly against me, rubbing her arms and willing the circulation back into her frozen limbs. Slowly, her shivers subsided, and she drew back from me with a grateful, if frightened, smile.

"Th-thanks," she said. "I suppose I sh-should have realized there'd be water by the b-bottom of the sub. What I did was st-stupid."

In a fit of reckless abandon, I grasped her chin with one hand and shook my head. Had I been a braver man, I may have kissed her…but I didn't. Instead, I asked her if she was okay before turning my attention to the *Aurora* and the pool she floated in.

It was roughly circular, with the mist covering most of it. I crouched down and wafted my hand through the haze, trying to clear it away. The water underneath was black and unforgiving. I leaned over to dip my outstretched fingers into it, but a sharp intake of breath from Ailsa made me stop just before I touched it.

"Look…" she breathed and pointed to the cavern walls.

Along their glassy surfaces, massive crystals I hadn't noticed before began to gleam. Their light refracted in the mist, causing a myriad of rainbows to form. Their colors were unlike anything I had ever experienced before—a living kaleidoscope. Beneath our feet, the algal mats writhed and sent up filaments to meet the colorful display. From these filaments, buds grew. One by one, they unfurled to expose bunches of delicate, red tentacles—not unlike anemones—which swayed as if caught in a breeze.

I held my breath, stunned. Some of the growths exceeded eight feet in height, turning the once bare cavern into a veritable forest. At their bases, small crab-like creatures crawled out of the mud and scuttled off, gathering the slime that grew upon the algae with viciously long claws. Our predicament momentarily forgotten, we wandered in this alien wonderland, exploring it as best we could. Alongside the crabs, there were other creatures that made Ailsa gasp in sheer astonishment. Trilobites, long thought extinct, paddled in the many pools of water, accompanied by something neither of us had ever seen before. It resembled a small, pale squid that supported itself upon five prehensile tentacles, which it used to squirm along the slippery ground. Near the roof of the cave, something huge soared over us on membranous wings. It shrieked once—a sound so grating that we both winced and covered our ears with our hands.

Ailsa, curious as ever about the rocks, carefully made her way to the walls. They were a deep, glossy black and studded with sizeable crystals. The largest of these crystals emanated the light—a gentle glow that came from their hearts. Carefully, she tapped at one with her spanner, hoping to loosen it from its surrounding matrix. After a few minutes of fierce concentration, it dropped into her hand. She held it up to the light and studied it closely. It was the size of her fist and vaguely octahedral in shape. With a gasp, she handed it to me.

"It's diamond. Pure diamond."

I gave her a disbelieving look.

"Seriously, Tom," she said. "It's absolutely flawless." She indicated to the rest of the wall with a flourish of her hand. "I would guess that all of these crystals are diamonds. A treasure trove of diamonds." Her voice lowered to a reverential whisper. "We must be in some kind of volcanic tube. A big one, too"

I marveled at the diamond in my hand, luxuriating in its cold weight. It had to be five times the size of the Hope diamond—and this was one of the *smaller* examples. Above us, precious gemstones the size of hubcaps glowed, and the points of light captured within their depths twinkled like stars.

Ailsa stuffed the oversized diamond into the pouch usually used for collecting rock specimens, and we continued on.

A soft, slapping noise from up ahead caught my attention. I stopped and listened—my head cocked like a deer sensing the circling wolf. The sound had a rhythmic quality to it...footsteps. Something let out a deep, guttural croak, and something else replied with a menacing hiss. The effect upon Ailsa was electric. Her eyes widened, and a hunted look stole over her. She grabbed my arm and pulled me down behind a clump of crimson fronds.

"Hey!" I said as I landed ass-first in the mud. She jabbed a finger at her pursed lips, her eyes silently begging me to be quiet.

There was another croak.

"What—" I began but stopped when Ailsa clapped her hand over my mouth and shook her head violently. I pulled her hand free and frowned. What was wrong with her?

What is that? I mouthed.

Ailsa said nothing. A series of strange barks echoed throughout the cavern. She flinched and burrowed herself as deeply as she could into the strange copse, her eyes huge and face pale.

"Ailsa—" I began and leaned forward to look through the fronds myself, but she shook her head so vehemently, I sat back and shut up immediately. It was then that I realized she was shaking. Not trembling but actually shaking. She cringed back against me, and we cowered together under the algal filaments, listening. The croaks receded and then disappeared altogether.

Still, we waited.

The light from the crystals began to wane. As it did, the filaments retreated, transforming the once blooming landscape into a stinking mudflat once again. Ailsa glanced about herself wildly, obviously looking for somewhere to hide, but there was nowhere—not that she had to hide. There was nothing else on the flats but us.

My curiosity won.

"What was that all about?" I said.

Ailsa rubbed the side of her face with her hand, a sure sign that she was nervous.

"I...I don't know. It's nothing." She shivered. "I just didn't feel up to facing something alive here."

Her excuse sounded flimsy, even to me.

"Are you sure it's nothing?" I asked. "You seem pretty freaked out."

"And you aren't? Tom, we are God-knows where with no real way of finding our way back." She wrapped her arms about herself. "I don't know about you, but I think keeping our presence here quiet is important."

"I don't know...it seemed more than that. Of course, I want to keep us as safe as possible, but you—"

"Look, just drop it, Tom. Drop it. I don't want to talk about it. Not here, not now. Especially not now. We need to concentrate on finding Brett."

She stalked off, and I studied her for a moment. I couldn't help but be alarmed at this abrupt change in her. She was usually the fearless one, the rational one, the one who balanced Brett and me out. To see her so...unbalanced was unnerving, to say the least. I decided not to push it. I ran after her.

"Okay, honey—"

"Don't you dare patronize me, Tom."

I smiled. That was more like it.

"Okay, Doctor MacDonald. We'll make our way back to the sub and see what we can do to get it working, again."

"No," she said. No? What did she mean by no? Did she want to *stay* here? "We can't leave Brett here."

Ah.

"Ailsa..."

"Don't 'Ailsa' me, Tom. The sub is fucked. You know that. How the hell we're still alive, I don't know. If we try to take it back down, the glass is going to give way. Even if by some miracle the glass holds, none of the kit works, including the re-breather. I wouldn't give us a snowflake's chance in hell of surviving."

Whether I liked it or not, she had a point.

"So, what do we do?" I asked.

"We find Brett," she said, as if it was the simplest thing in the world. "Then, we try to find another way out. If this is a volcanic tube, there has to be a way up somewhere."

She made it all sound so simple, but I knew differently.

"Where exactly do we start looking?"

"Over there might be a good idea."

I followed her line of sight and almost fell over backward. In the distance, the wall of the cavern looked like it had a massive set of stairs carved into it. How I hadn't noticed them before, I'll never know.

"I don't know about a 'good idea,'" I said, "but it looks like an idea." I offered her my hand, which she took gratefully. Together, we slapped through the mud toward the staircase.

After about half an hour, the ground grew firmer beneath our feet, and the general landscape felt a little tamer. Not much, but a little. We stopped by the foot of the staircase, and I looked up, awed by their sheer size. Rather like the pillars, they were made of interlocking blocks whose geometry seemed ever so slightly out of kilter, so much so that when I tried to clamber up I misjudged it and barked my shin painfully against its edge.

"Careful, clumsy," Ailsa said and chuckled nervously. She then tried to take a step and nearly fell flat on her face. "What the..."

"I know. It's weird. Something's not right with the...the...I don't know. The dimensions?" I paused for a moment to take in the titanic construction. "How on earth did they build this?"

My question was more for myself than Ailsa, but nevertheless, she shrugged and gave me a worried look.

"I think that's the wrong question, Tom... maybe we should be asking *who* built this."

In the end, we found it easier to climb with our eyes shut, feeling our way up. What we saw and what we felt were so disparate that, on one occasion, I swore I saw my fingers actually sink into the rock before I touched it. Upon reaching the top, I glanced back and nearly collapsed in astonishment. We had climbed, I don't know, around twelve steps?—but from where we stood, it looked like we had climbed over a mile, the mist-wreathed swamp no more than a garden plot below us.

I felt a tug on my sleeve. Ailsa handed me something made of a dark, canvas-like material. Brett's backpack. I took it from her and rummaged inside. It was full—rations, wallet, flash light, safety gear, the lot. Wherever he had gone, he had obviously decided he didn't need it.

"Well, at least we know he was here," Ailsa said.

"Yes," I said. "But where has he gone?"

Ailsa looked over her shoulder. Behind her stood a pair of monolithic doors that seemed carved out of the very rock itself. They were unadorned and open just enough to allow someone to squeeze through the gap.

I ran a hand through my hair.

"Looks like we know where he went after all," I said.

Ailsa nodded slowly but didn't say anything. I couldn't blame her. I didn't really want to make the suggestion, either.

"Then, I guess we have no choice." I shouldered Brett's backpack, and without another word—mainly because I knew if I said anything else, I'd lose my nerve—I squeezed through the gap in the doors and into the unknown darkness beyond.

Chapter Four

I'm not too ashamed to admit that it took me a little while to muster the courage to step fully into the room beyond those doors. Going through them somehow confirmed what was happening to us; the cold weight of the rock under my hands as I squeezed through that gap made my scalp crawl in a way I usually reserved solely for large spiders and immense heights. There was something about its sheer size that intimidated me, and all the while, a little niggle at the back of my mind kept up a barrage of questions I had no hope of answering.

I was expecting the room to be big, but I wasn't expecting it to be quite *that* big. It was easily the size of your average football field, and I had the uneasy feeling that somehow, the space inside this...building? Construction? I didn't know what to call it, if I'm honest—didn't really fit the outside dimensions, but how that could be, I had no idea.

The lighting didn't help. What meager light there was, it was an eldritch green, lending everything a sickly cast. It took a while for my eyesight to adjust to the gloom, and even then, I wasn't exactly sure what I was looking at.

I hesitated to call them statues. While there was some semblance of form to them, I had to screw my eyes up to see it. They were of all shapes and sizes, and they filled the room. A few of them even stretched to the barely visible ceiling, forming immense pillars. They filled the hall, the further ones distorted to the point of hurting my eyes.

Ailsa and I wandered amongst them in silence, sharing troubled looks. Like the stairs outside, what we saw wasn't necessarily the same as what we felt, and there were a few occasions when I thought I should be touching solid rock, when in fact my fingers were still groping through the frigid air.

"This place is giving me a headache," Ailsa said.

I nodded in return. This place was giving me a headache, too. A nasty little uneasy pain just between my eyes.

In the end, the only way we found we could find our way around was to track one of the walls until we found a door.

In complete contrast to the entrance, the exit from the antechamber was small and plain. A blast of cold air, its scent reminding me of Arctic waters, drew me to it. Apart from the incessant drip of water, all was quiet.

Nervously, I pushed the door open. Nothing stirred. I waited. Still, nothing stirred. I waited a little bit more. Still, nothing sti—

"Tom...are we standing here for any particular reason?" Ailsa whispered.

I swallowed hard, offered her a slightly embarrassed smile, and stepped through the doorway.

A corridor lay on the other side. Much to our relief, its dimensions played nice, and by mutual agreement, we crept along silently, keeping to the walls. Other doors were dotted around, but every single one was stuck fast. Even a good whack with Ailsa's spanner wouldn't dislodge them. Eventually, the corridor transformed into a tunnel-like structure, its walls studded with gemstones that sparkled by the light of our headlamps. The floor was uneven and dotted with pools of stagnant brine and a slippery, purple slime. We continued on carefully until our progress was halted by a huge, iron door, rusted by the ages. I grasped the door handle and gave it a good shove, but like the others, it was stuck fast.

"Well...that's that. None of the doors work. What now?" I asked.

Ailsa swept her flashlight over the walls. Just above our heads, the beam picked up the gaping maws of other, smaller tunnels that branched off at haphazard angles. They weren't nearly so regular as the main tunnel, and a fresh burst of anxiety swept through me when Ailsa grabbed one of the protruding gemstone nodules and began to climb.

"Hey, hey! What do you think you're doing?" I asked.

"Having a look," she said.

"Just having a look? Ailsa, there could be anything up there."

"Oh, come on, Tom. There's nothing here—"

"There's nothing here that we can see."

"There's nothing here, and we have no choice. Where else are we supposed to go? I'm the geologist. At least let me take a look."

I pursed my lips, unhappy at the whole situation. She had a point. There was nowhere else to look, but that didn't mean

I had to like it. I dug my hand into my pocket and pulled out a coin.

"Okay...flip you for it."

"What?"

"I'll flip you for it. Heads, I go first. Tails, you do. Sound fair?"

"If it makes you happy. Only I want heads." She grinned at me, and I rolled my eyes at her.

"All right. You go on heads, I go on tails."

I balanced the coin on my fingertips and flicked my thumb up. It spun into the air with a faint twang, and then tumbled down into my waiting hand. With baited breath, I slapped it onto the back of my other hand.

Heads.

"There you go," Ailsa said. "I'll go look."

I didn't like it. I didn't like it one bit. I thought of refusing to let her go, but we'd agreed, and I knew that if I muscled in now, she'd never forgive me. I bit the inside of my cheek to stop myself from pulling her away from the wall and watched as she ran her hand around the edge of one of the larger tunnels. It was three, possibly four feet in diameter and large enough to admit a person...if they crawled.

"Lots of purple stuff in here," she said. "What is it?"

"I don't know," I said, trying to sound calm. *Just pull her away from the wall. Go on. Screw the fact that you'll piss her off. Just do it!* "Some kind of microbial mat, maybe?"

"Maybe..." Ailsa wiped her hand clean on her thigh and continued to study the tunnel. "This is weird. This doesn't look like a natural hole. It looks like the rock has been bored into."

"Bored into?"

"Yeah. Like a big drill or something."

"Could be some kind of bivalve? There are some species that bore into rock," I said, and then laughed at my own foolishness. "Of course, this one would have to be an eight-foot monster to make a tunnel that size..."

"Now *that* would be a discovery!" She ran her hand along the inside of the opening again and then wiped it on her thigh "I'm going to take a look. It may lead us somewhere else."

"What if there *is* a giant mollusk at the end of it all?" I asked, trying to remain lighthearted.

"Then, my name will go down in history!" she replied

with a grin and a flourish of her hand. I tried to grin back but couldn't help but notice the humorous tone in her voice was forced.

I knew what she was doing. She was willing to risk everything just on the off chance it might get us out of this strange nightmare. I loathed myself for allowing her to take the lead as I waited outside the mouth of the tunnel. At first, she gave me a running commentary of her progress—how the tunnel sides were damp and covered in a strange, iridescent matter that glowed purple in the light of her torch, that the diameter of the tunnel remained constant and seemed to sloped downward. The further she moved away, the less distinct her voice became, until it vanished altogether.

Alone in the circular corridor, my formless fears finally made a leap of faith to the realms of full-blown panic. I shouldn't have let her go. I should have gone with her. I should never have let her go. What was I thinking? Once three, then two...now one? What if she got stuck? What if my half-hearted joke about an undiscovered species lying in wait for unwary travelers was true?

What if she never came back?

I grasped the edge of the tunnel again and hauled myself up to peer into the darkness ahead of me.

"Ailsa?"

Nothing.

"Ailsa!" I tried again, louder this time, my voice a good octave higher than normal.

I lowered myself down and chewed the inside of my cheek, paralyzed. One thing was certain. Ailsa was braver than me. Just the sight of that dark mouth leading to God knows where was enough to make my balls want to climb back inside me. Even so, the little voice wouldn't let up. I should have gone. Some gentleman I was. Then again, she won the coin flip... but no. That was just an excuse. I should have gone. I should have gone.

A shrill scream drilled through my train of thought.

"Ailsa!" I tried to shout, but it came out as a feeble croak. My heart thumping wildly, I heaved myself into the opening. It was slippery inside, and I slid part of the way on my belly, using the slime to lubricate my passage before my hands and knees caught up with me.

Another scream, this time followed by a distant splash.

"A-Ailsa!"

A gust of fetid air rolled down the tunnel. I choked, and my hands slid forward, leaving me floundering in the filth once again. Ahead of me, the tunnel seemed to shrink, its walls constricting me. I felt the dead weight of the rocks above me. The sheer enormity of geological time used to create the bedrock pressed down upon my fragile body until my lungs threatened to burst. I fought to take in a breath but couldn't. I scrabbled at my throat, trying to locate my mouthpiece, but in my panic, I pitched forward and banged my head upon an unexpected nodule.

My headlamp guttered and died.

If I thought the blackness of the deep-sea was absolute, it was nothing compared to this. Suffocating in the dark, I tried to shout out, but I could only utter a thin squeak. I began to shake all over—not just a minor tremble but proper convulsions as my body attempted to make the space around me larger. A small, detached part of me—the same part that floated away when the *Aurora* was incapacitated—realized that I was panicking to the point of hysteria. I gave myself a stern nudge. All I had to do was get the light working. That was all. Just get the light working.

I took in as deep a breath as I could manage and reached up, my hands shaking. It took three attempts for me to grasp the band that secured the lamp and pull it from my brow. I shifted round onto my back and smacked the lamp with the palm of my hand. It flickered to life briefly, only to die once again.

"No...no...just work!" I moaned.

I smacked it, again. Again, it flickered and died.

"Fuck! No! Just come on. *Work!*"

All around me, the rock began to vibrate.

I sobbed in fear, my mind feeding my terror with imagined monstrosities of the deep, and I grappled again with my headlamp. I gave it one last desperate thump, and I almost cried when it gave in an allowed me a sickly, yellow beam. It wasn't enough to light up the tunnel, but it was just enough to banish the oppressive darkness. I lay in the tunnel for a moment longer, fighting down the urge to scramble backward and get the hell out of Dodge. In the end, my duty toward Ailsa won. I turned back onto my belly and peered ahead of me. About five feet ahead of me, the tunnel branched.

"Ailsa!" I squeaked.

There was no reply.

I crawled toward the junction, praying to find some trace of her. The left tunnel was a lot narrower than the right, and my mouth, already claggy, ran dry. *Please...not the left-hand side, not the left-hand side, not the left...*

I took a moment to study each entrance and spotted what looked like handprints marred by drag marks in the slime of the right-hand tunnel—crawl marks. I almost felt relieved by this. Almost.

I continued to commando-crawl forward, muttering snatches of the nursery rhymes I had sung to my son as a baby to calm my nerves. It had been a long time since I'd seen him. He was now a teenager with no time for dear old Dad. I stopped for a moment. Why was I thinking about him at a time like this? His mother's face loomed in front of me out of the darkness, and for a moment, I cowered as she berated me within the confines of my mind. "No good. Never has been. Always away. No time for us," she screamed...and she was right. I pushed the heels of my sludge-covered hands into my eye sockets and willed the thoughts away, knowing that between them and the agonizing claustrophobia of the tunnel lay a madness so acute, I would never resurface.

When I removed my hands, my headlamp died again, and this time, I did scream. I fancied I heard an answering call. *Please, Ailsa. Let it be Ailsa*, my mind gibbered, and I began back up, out of the tunnel. I couldn't do this. There had to be another way.

A flash of scintillating lights caught my eye.

They glittered ahead of me like jewels in firelight, their colors forming coruscating trails against the infinite blackness. I was reminded of the strange inhabitants of the deep—the cone jellies, the tiny copepods, the jewel octopi, and all their bioluminescent ilk. I watched as the lights bobbed and span, dancing in the darkness, their beguiling whimsy making me smile—

My smile froze as my mind backed up a bit. What had I thought? Cone jellies, copepods, octopi and their bioluminescent ilk...

Bioluminescent.

Bio.

Bio meant life.

Life meant something was alive in the tunnel.

Adrenaline, hot and fluid, flooded my system. The lights continued blinking, closer and closer. I tried to force my limbs to move, but they were like jelly. A slow, slurping noise stole over the thudding of my heart, and the fetor grew until the stench of mud and decay stung my eyes.

Instinctively, I knew what the slime that coated the walls—that coated *me*—was. It wasn't algae or any form of microbial life. It was the excreta. Whatever the glittering, amorphous thing was ahead of me, I was floundering in its shit.

The lights drew ever closer, giving the creature an outline—an outline that changed, its form bubbling and shifting like the smokers out on the abyssal plain. I skittered backward on my hands and knees just as the thing threw a pseudopod made of some transparent matter toward me. It grazed the back of my hand, and I felt its acidic bite. I yelped—a high, girlish sound—and I continued to back away.

The creature now filled the entire tunnel. Even this close, I couldn't make out its true nature. Its surface boiled with innumerable colors, all of them beautiful. All over its body, I saw flickers of what looked like eyes—huge and staring—and puckered mouths, full of needle-pointed teeth, form and then melt away before my very eyes.

The sensation of space behind me told me I had reached the branch, again. The monster threw more tendrils of the viscous matter that made it up in my direction, trying to cut off my escape. I tried to back off further, and my hand, once securely planted on slick rock, fell into nothing. I had found the opening to the left tunnel.

It was dry.

I didn't stop to think why or worry about the fact that it was smaller than the main tunnel. Dry meant no slime. No slime meant no excreta. For whatever reason, the blob didn't go down this particular tunnel, which meant it was as good as any haven for me. I gasped in agony as another acidic pseudopod caught my shoulder and ate through the thick material of my environment suit. I threw myself down the left tunnel and wriggled like a snake, all the while praying that my hunch was right. Turns out it was...up to a point. The creature sent out a couple of feelers after me, but it didn't follow. Not that I cared. It wasn't following, and that's all that mattered.

I didn't even get the time to scream when the tunnel

suddenly pitched steeply forward. There was nothing I could do, nothing to hold on to that would stop me from tumbling down a hole the darkness had hidden all along.

Chapter Five

My plunge was so dark, for a split second, it felt as if I was floating.

Then, I hit the freezing water below.

The impact forced the breath from my lungs, my limbs to seize, my heart to stop in my chest.

So cold.

I sank. My mind conjured countless, jumbled images as panic took hold of me. Arms flailing, I desperately sought the surface, but I had nothing to guide my way. Up, down, left, right—they didn't exist. Something brushed past my foot, and I screamed. Frigid water flooded my mouth, tracking a burning path to my lungs. I wanted to cough, to expel the fire while little, purple lights of hypoxia began to dance in front of my eyes. Was this it? Was this the end? No. It couldn't be. I had to find Ailsa. I had to find her. It was my fault she entered the tunnel first. It was the least I could do. With one last, furious kick, I propelled myself forward, and with a relief that almost eclipsed orgasm, I finally broke the surface of the water.

I pulled in breath after glorious breath until I felt giddy. I lay back in the water, and a laugh bubbled from my lips. I was alive! Alive!

Alive, but alone.

Dread pummeled me back down to earth. Yes, I was alive... but where was Ailsa?

I thought of the thing in the tunnel above. Was she now nothing more than purple slime? What about whatever brushed against my leg in the water? Now, my mind tortured me with images of Ailsa scrabbling at me, trying to find something—anything—to grasp and maybe stop herself from drowning, but I had brushed her off.

Had I killed her?

"Ailsa!" I cried out in a rasping voice. "*Ailsa!*"

In the distance—I don't know from what direction-came an answering call.

"Tom!"

I don't think I can describe the joy, the wonder, or the sheer fucking elation I felt at hearing her voice.

"Ailsa!" I called out again, just to make sure I wasn't hallucinating.

A light, pure and white, shone to my left.

"Tom! Swim to me!"

I laughed and lay back in the water, tears of relief rolling down my cheeks. Ailsa was still alive. She was okay. That meant everything else was okay.

"Tom! Get out of the water! Get out of the water, now!"

I hauled myself upright and tread water, feeling confused. She should be happy. She was alive. So, why did she sound terrified. What was going—

Something bumped against my foot.

I'm a strong swimmer. I swam for the swim team at the university. I'd even won championships, but that was nothing compared to how I moved now. My strokes were undisciplined and messy, but sheer terror gave them a strength I had never experienced before. The light drew closer, and the sound of splashing up ahead told me Ailsa was also in the water, trying to reach me. Finally, I caught sight of her blessed face. I grabbed her outstretched hand, and she hauled me from the water.

As she did so, I felt a rush behind me. I don't know how I knew—call it instinct—but something was charging me. Patterns of scintillating lights and ever-changing, translucent flesh surfaced in my mind's eye. Ailsa screamed again and yanked me as hard as she could toward the shore. I stumbled in the shallows, and the water washed over me again. I staggered up, coughing. All the while, Ailsa kept tugging on my arm, her eyes as round as headlamps. I glanced behind myself only to catch sight of something massive rearing out of the water, then splash back into the depths once again.

We sprinted together out of the shallow water and onto the sand. We didn't stop until the sand beneath our feet ran out, and we hit a sheer rock face.

Ailsa let out a sob and threw her arms around me. I tried to compose myself—to be the man—but I couldn't hold my tears back. I hugged her back, and the urge—monstrous and primal—to throw her up against the cliff face and celebrate just how good it felt to be alive suddenly rose within me. Within moments, my mouth found hers. She did not shy away and allowed my desperate lips to ravage hers, hungry for her very humanity. My wayward hand instinctively rose to cup a breast flattened by her environment suit, and she moaned against me as my thumb found a nipple straining against the constricting fabric.

A screeching cry brought us both to our senses. Our bodies, so grateful for being allowed to live, cried out to celebrate this fact. Our minds, ever aware of the constant threat of this alien place, froze our libidinous urges. Ailsa gave me a frightened look, and that was enough. I took her hand, and together, we skirted the edge of the rocks, looking for somewhere to take shelter.

* * * *

It took us a while to inspect the cave-riddled cliff face that bordered the beach. We avoided the deeper ones. Who knew what lived in those dark holes. Instead, we decided to take shelter in one of the smaller caves. It wasn't much more than a fissure in the rock, but we hoped it would be enough protect us from prying—and possibly predatory—eyes. We sat together on the sand, our headlamps the only light source.

"What do you think that thing in the water was?" Ailsa asked.

I shrugged.

"Who knows?" Talking to Ailsa felt awkward now, as if I was a teenager again, faced with my first kiss. "It was completely unlike that thing in the tunnel, though. Alongside everything else, it looks like they have a whole, self-sustaining ecosystem down here."

"Yeah, a self-sustaining ecosystem of nightmarish horror," Ailsa muttered. She then gave me an inquiring look. "What thing in the tunnel?" She readjusted her ponytail, and I tried to ignore the way her breasts changed shape as she lifted her arms. *Just a natural reaction*, I told myself. Nothing more. A natural reaction to danger. One of the many "F's"—fight, flight, freeze, fart, fawn, and fuck.

As if reading my mind, she dropped her arms and drew her knees up to her chin. She still couldn't make eye contact with me.

"The jelly thing in the tunnel," I said. "It had lights. It tried to...well, I don't know what it was trying to do. Engulf me, I suppose. I heard you scream. I kind of assumed you'd come across it, too."

"Nope. I explored a bit of the right tunnel, but it was really sticky in there, so I decided to try the left hand side out, instead. I screamed when I fell down the hole. Maybe, I woke it up." She looked worried.

"No, no. I don't think you did," I said, perhaps a little more quickly than I should have. "I mean, I don't think it sleeps like we do. It was unlike anything I've ever seen before. At first, I thought it was some kind of gelatinous algae, but then, it moved. All I could do was try to get away from it." I paused. "I was worried it got you. Really worried."

Ailsa said nothing. She continued to watch the water for a while and then rubbed her eyes with the back of her hand.

"Where the hell are we, Tom?" she whispered. The slight hitch in her voice betrayed the tears she was trying so hard to hide. "What in God's name is going on?"

I moved toward her and sat down, offering her my shoulder. She hesitated for a moment but took it with a small smile of gratitude, laying her damp head next to my cheek.

"I don't know," I answered. I could've tried to make up some pseudo-scientific mumbo jumbo to comfort her, but I respected her too much for that. "I don't dare guess, either."

Something massive and dark surfaced again in the lagoon. The dim light of our headlamps did nothing to quell our fears. If anything, the shadows our lights created distorted its bulk, making it seem even more terrible than before.

"It's watching us," Ailsa said quietly. "After I fell in, it circled me and sized me up. When I got out of the water, I could hear it splashing around. I'm sure it was raising its head above the water, so it could look at me." She shivered.

"It was probably just trying to figure out where its meal had gone," I said, a little too heartily.

"No...something else was going on. It had scars on it. Quite long ones. I think it was afraid of me. Just a little bit. That's why it didn't attack right away."

I thought of the amorphous blob inhabiting the tunnels above it. Maybe, it had a good reason to be afraid.

There was another splash, this time closer to the shore. Just as Ailsa said, I got the distinct feeling it was watching us. It knew we weren't a threat, now. We could be friends. It could help us. Just step into the water. Step into the water...

I made to stand up. Ailsa tugged at my arm, and I shook my head sharply. What was I doing?

"It's getting to you, too, huh?"

I didn't answer and just gave her a bewildered look.

She snorted.

"A psychic sea monster...who would've thought?"

"Legends are full of men being lured to their deaths in the depths," I said. "Mermaids, sirens, the Kraken—"

"The Kraken hardly lured men into the depths," Ailsa said.

"Really? Then, why do so many people go hunting it? Do you have any idea how many people have died in pursuit of such cryptids?"

"I suppose you have a point," she said.

"Anyway, it's no stranger than the murderous, not-quite-a-jellyfish-but-I-think-I'll-call-it-that-anyway-because-thinking-too-much-about-it-might-make-me-go-ever-so-slightly-nuts," I said.

Ailsa laughed again, and I think that's when the sad, little crush I had on her turned to true love.

"That's one hell of a name," she said. "What would that be in Latin?"

I thought for a moment.

"An *Amorphousi whothehellknowsidae*?" I grinned.

The smile that graced her strained features was wide and genuine, and it enhanced the fragility held within her eyes. Again, I fought the desire to cup her cheeks and kiss her over and over, until all I could think about was her. Instead, we sat in silence, trying to ignore the siren call of the creature in the water. Eventually, Ailsa grabbed Brett's backpack and started to rummage around. She pulled out a jumble of stuff— a sweater, a small gas canister, two more chemical flares, a leather wallet, a water canister, and a small vacuum pack of field rations. As she tore into the silvery wrappings, I picked up the wallet.

She offered me a dry cracker and indicated to the wallet.

"Why on earth would Brett take that with him? I mean, it's not as if they accept MasterCard down here."

"I know," I said. I took a cracker, not because I was hungry, but more because the act of eating allowed me to focus on something simple, something wholesome. I flicked open the wallet. Inside were the usual array of credit cards and a few damp notes tucked into one of the pockets, as well as a creased photo of a girl around sixteen years of age, and a folded newspaper clipping.

Ailsa took the photo from me. After studying it for a moment, she flipped it over.

"Marissa," she said and shrugged. "Wasn't that his sister's name?"

I shook my head and carefully unfolded the clipping. It was old. The paper felt soft and fragile, its creases well defined. It read:

1st March 1996
Day of the Lost
There have been reports from all over the world of mass disappearances following a freak, low-frequency sound that was recorded in the South Pacific Ocean. The disappearances were confined to coastal regions, and the world over, authorities are struggling to understand what has occurred. Some have speculated mass hysteria leading to mass suicide, but the sheer scope of the disappearances means most experts think this unlikely; however, the lack of any other answers means—

A nonsensical string of made-up words obscured the rest of the article. They looped around one another, forming spirals, rendering them virtually unreadable. The only word I could make out with any certainty was "Marissa", which was repeated over and over again in the margins of the article.

Wordlessly, I handed the article to Ailsa.

"Hey, I remember that day," she said. "Loads of people went missing."

I nodded. I remembered that day as well. It was one of those things you didn't really forget.

"I wonder what happened to all those people." Ailsa continued. "They reckon the final tally of the missing reached thousands. They can't even say they died, because no one found any bodies. How can thousands of people just disappear like that, completely and utterly without a trace?" She read the article, again. By the way she screwed her eyes up, I guessed she was trying to make out the bits obscured by Brett's strange scribblings. "He's written that name all over the place." She looked at the photo, again. "Marissa. I wonder why he wrote her name all over this."

I knew the game she was playing and was grateful. Anything to distract us from what was happening. I took the photo from her. "She has his nose," I said. "I think you're probably right. Looks like she could be his sister."

"Didn't she die or something?" Ailsa said.

"Yeah—I think she drowned, but I'm not sure."

"Yeah, he mentioned something about that to me once, too. He told me she had disappeared, though."

"Marissa...what happened to you?" I murmured, turning the photo over in my hands. "Are you one of the Lost?"

"Heh, might explain Brett's strange obsession with people living under the sea," she said.

"So, he mentioned that to you as well, huh?"

"Oh, yes. Ancient gods slumbering under the ocean floor, waiting for the stars to be right so they could awaken, and, well...I don't know, to be honest. I kind of stopped listening to him."

"Yeah...me, too." I put the photo back into Brett's wallet and spent a moment taking in the scenery. "Although, I kind of get the feeling maybe we should have been paying attention to him after all."

Ailsa shivered.

"You know...you could be right."

We both sat in strained silence, again. For the first time in my life, I'd never wished to be more wrong. Yet, here we were, trapped in a place God only knew where, with no hope of ever finding our way home. As if sensing my mounting despair, Ailsa picked up the water canister. She took a swig and then offered it to me.

"Not too much, mind you. We've got to make that last."

I smiled at her and took just enough to rinse my mouth.

"Shame it's not something stronger," I said.

"When you're right, you're right, Tom," she agreed.

Again, our conversation faltered, and silence returned. I found myself wondering yet again what she would do if I leaned over and kissed her.

"We should move," I said instead.

"We should," Ailsa agreed.

We didn't.

Chapter Six

I wish I could now regale you with tales of how Ailsa and I threw caution to the wind and made wild, passionate love on that prehistoric beach, like some kind of deep-sea *From Here to Eternity*. I wish I could recount how sweet her mouth felt against mine, how delicious it felt to slide myself into her, and how wonderful her skin felt under my roaming hands.

I wish I could, but I can't.

We didn't do any of that. Instead, we did nothing more than sit and watch the sinister waves lap at the sand, each lost in a world of our own.

After a while, Ailsa stood up—to shake the pins and needles from her legs, or so she claimed—and I knew it was time to go. I swallowed down any secret longings I harbored and joined her. Together, we scoped out the other caves along the coastline, looking for a passage that would take us away from that terrible beach, until a dreadful smell stopped us in our tracks.

"What is that?" Ailsa asked, covering her nose and mouth with one hand.

"I don't know. Smells like something died...maybe, a whale?" I glanced toward the water. "Or something like it?"

"Let's hope that whatever it is actually *is* dead," she said.

I was going to comment that very few things stink like that when alive. Then, I thought of the thing in the tunnels above us, and an icy shudder ran the length of my spine. Who knew in this place?

I steeled myself and stalked toward the source of the smell, trying to ignore the sick feeling that settled over me. Ailsa followed, albeit a little reluctantly. The stench grew to almost unbearable levels until a large shape loomed out of the gloom. I stopped, my heart jackhammering in my chest. I waited for any signs of movement, but there were none. My jittery mind connected the obvious dots. It didn't move, because it was dead. Of course, it was dead.

I cracked open a flare and raised it above my head. The

red light it produced made everything look like it had been drenched in blood, and for a moment, I wished I hadn't bothered. I took a deep breath and approached the carcass slowly. It was enormous, easily nearing fifty feet in length from snout to tail. Its heavy bulk was already beginning to rupture as the gases trapped within made a bid for freedom. My gorge rose, and I covered my hand and nose with one hand, copying Ailsa. No matter how many times I saw dead things rotting on beaches, I never got used to the smell. I heard a retching sound behind me. Should I help her or allow her some measure of dignity? In the end, her dignity won out, but not through any form of chivalry on my part. I was struggling enough not to puke, and the last thing I needed was to witness anyone else being sick.

"Are you okay?" I managed to ask.

"Yes...yes, sorry." Her voiced sounded tight and heavy, and I knew she was still fighting her nausea. I heard the sound of her boots crunching on the sand behind me. "Dear Lord, that's an unholy stench!"

"Understatement of the year," I said. I turned back to her and offered her a reassuring smile. "At least it confirms that it is indeed dead."

"Thank the Lord for small mercies, I suppose" she said and drew level with me. "But what is it?" She peered forward and then dropped her hand and gasped. "It looks like a pliosaur, but how can that be?"

I glanced at her, disbelief furrowing my brow. Of course, I knew what a pliosaur was. At the university, I served my time studying the ancient creatures of the deep as well as the ones swimming around. Even with all I had previously seen, I could not quite take it in that this decaying monster was one believed to be extinct for 100 million years.

I left Ailsa to circle the beast, so I could see it in all its rotting glory. As soon as I saw its head, I knew Ailsa was right. It was huge and hideously reptilian, its eyes almost vestigial—an adaptation for living in these darkest of waters, I guessed—and its teeth beyond massive. All over its mottled body were scars. Some old, some fresh, but what made them, I couldn't tell.

The flare in my hand sputtered and died, and we were once again left to rely upon our headlamps. Their thin beams did nothing to illuminate the corpse before us. Again, they merely enhanced the shadows, turning the corpse into something even more mysterious and monstrous. The temptation to enter the water hit me again, and a splash told me our gargantuan friend remained out there, waiting. A cracking sound made my heart stutter, but then, another flare glowed to life, and I realized it was just Ailsa relighting another stick. She gave me a nervous smile and held it high above her head.

"Sorry. I couldn't bear the thought of being here, near this...creature without a decent light source," she said. She paused and then gestured her head toward the sea. "Can you feel it?"

I knew exactly what she meant. I nodded.

"It seems lonely."

"I know."

"Do you think this was its mate?"

I turned my attention back to the stinking carcass.

"Maybe." I began to inspect its scars. "You know, these look almost like the same scars sport fish get when people go spear fishing..." I ground my teeth to stop the rising tide of nausea as I reached forward to touch the would-be pliosaur and pulled the lips of a fresh-looking wound apart.

Something glittered within its depths.

I took a step back, pulled my pocket knife from my belt, and took in a deep breath.

The blade of the knife slid into the creature's flesh far too easily. A small trickle of putrescence ran down the side of its body as I twisted the knife. Something long and slender protruded from the wound. Gagging a little, I grasped it and tried to pull it free. After a couple of tugs, it slipped out with an unpleasant sucking sound.

"What is it?" Ailsa asked, her face a picture of disgust.

"I don't know," I replied. I wandered the short distance to the water's edge.

"Tom..." Ailsa warned.

"It's okay. I'm just going to clean it," I said.

The overwhelming urge to enter the water grew again as I washed the artifact. It would have been so easy to just keep going, to swim away forever and ever and ev—I jerked my gaze away from the water and forced myself to concentrate on the task at hand. Bits of putrid flesh floated away, revealing a serrated, metal shaft about six inches in length.

A spearhead.

My blood ran cold.

"Tom..." Ailsa said again, but this time, it wasn't in warning. If anything, she sounded even more frightened than before. I turned around and found her crouched down, studying something in the damp sand on the far side of the carcass. "I think you should come and have a look at this."

"What is it?"

"Just...just come and have a look."

I wandered over to her, spearhead in hand, and hunkered down beside her. She pointed wordlessly to a depression in the sand. It was triangular in shape with three points at the wider end.

I looked up and gave her a quizzical look. She said nothing and pointed along the beach.

There was another...and another...and another. All in a straight line. Then, it hit me.

Footprints.

"What did you find?" Ailsa asked.

I handed her the spearhead, and she took it from me with a trembling hand.

"Is that a..." She didn't finish.

"Yes. It's a spearhead." Ailsa, looking white, dropped the spearhead and wiped her hands on her thighs. We looked at one another. Someone—or something, judging by the shape of the footprints—was hunting huge, aquatic reptiles. With spears. My mouth ran dry.

"Maybe, we should carry on?" I asked.

Ailsa nodded quickly.

"Good idea. Just...let's not follow the footprints. Not unless we absolutely have to."

We carried on walking up the beach, away from the footprints. Once upon a time, we would have been bursting with curiosity as to where they led and who made them, but not now. Not after all we had been through. The beach soon ran out, forcing us to clamber over dark, slick boulders until our efforts were foiled by an extensive stretch of sheer rock. For all we knew, it rose up to join the roof of the cave above us. Ailsa swore under her breath. We were rapidly running out of options. Having no other choice, we turned back toward the beach and the dead behemoth that lay upon it.

It looked like we were going to have to follow the footprints, after all.

On my way past, I scooped up the cleaned spearhead, just in case. Just in case of what, I don't know, but for some reason, I felt a little better with its dead weight in my hand.

We continued to follow the tracks until they disappeared into what was more a crack in the rock than a true cave. Beyond its mouth lay a winding tunnel—not circular, much to our relief, but natural. Upon the sandy floor, the footprints continued. We carried on until the floor began to slope upward, and we reached what looked like a rope bridge spanning a deep chasm.

"Oh, my God. How deep is it?"

"I have no idea," I said.

Ailsa picked up a stone and dropped it into the chasm. We waited, counting the seconds down. When we reached ten, our alarm grew. When we reached fifteen, we stopped counting.

"That's ridiculous," she said. "Even taking the atmospherics here into consideration—"

"I know," I said. We should have heard something. That we didn't meant one thing. The hole was so deep, we couldn't hear the stone strike the bottom.

Either that, or there was no bottom for it to strike.

I swallowed hard and focused my attention upon the bridge. The planks were made of bones and the knotted rope that bound them together smelled of seaweed. I tested the first plank gingerly. The bridge creaked a little but held my weight.

"Tom...what are you doing?" Ailsa asked.

"We have to cross. It's not like we have any other choice. There is literally no other way."

"But that pit—"

"—is potentially bottomless? Yes, I know. Either way, we can't stay here."

She swallowed audibly and nodded. This time, she didn't argue to go first. She watched me as I skittered across the void, my heart in my mouth. I didn't dare look down once. I don't know what I was trying to prove—maybe, I was trying to make up for my cowardice before, in the tunnel. Whatever it was, and wherever it came from, I was grateful for it. Without it, I don't think I could have made it. Underneath me, cold air currents rushed up, bringing with them an odd smell of sulfur and something less definable. I was grateful to reach the other side and signaled for Ailsa to follow.

Despite her fearless nature, especially when it came to heights, she was wary. More than wary. In fact, if I didn't know her better, I'd say she was downright terrified. She clung onto the ropes that made up the bridge's balustrade for dear life. Halfway along, she stopped and looked down.

My heart gave one huge thump in my chest.

"Ailsa..." I tried to sound encouraging, but my voice came out as a thin croak. I tried, again. "Ailsa—don't stop, now. Just keep going. One foot in front of the other. Come on. Focus."

She didn't move or even make to acknowledge me. Little tendrils of fear plucked tunes of terror within me.

"Ailsa," I said again, my rising hysteria making me sound sharper than I intended. "Come on, girl. Keep going. Just keep going..."

She didn't, though. Instead, she leaned over the edge of the bridge.

"Ailsa!" I squawked, petrified, but it was obvious she didn't hear me. She just continued to peer into the darkness below, as if transfixed upon something in the deep.

"Look..." she breathed. "Down there. So beautiful..."

I followed her line of sight, and at first saw nothing. Then, something caught my eye—a ripple of scintillating colors in the darkness...

My gut twisted.

"Ailsa—get away!" I barked and stepped back onto the bridge. Ailsa leaned out further, one hand outstretched. She giggled.

"Stop it...please..." I knew full well what waited for her down there. I glanced back down—the lights seemed nearer, the smell more pronounced. I crabbed further back along the bridge, my legs feeling as if they were made of elastic bands, to pull her back.

She looked up at me, her expression slack.

"They go on forever..."

"That's right, Ailsa. Don't look at them. Look at me. Look at Tom. Don't look dow— Ailsa!"

She looked back, this time leaning so far over the rope balustrade that her feet left the planks. I dashed forward and made a grab at her ankle. My hand scrabbled at her skin and managed to catch the edge of her boot. She hung there, over that eon-deep chasm, teetering. Just one false move, and she would plunge down, down into the darkness, into the lair of that bubbling mess of flesh and light. I braced myself against the edge of the rope bridge and yanked her back as hard as I could. She slithered back and fell heavily against me, her legs buckling beneath her. I looked down, again. The lights were even closer, flashing, spinning, forming dazzling patterns of such beauty...

I shook my head sharply and gathered her up into my arms. She was now senseless. I half carried, half dragged her back to solid ground. I took a mere second to readjust my grip upon her and ran forward, away from the bridge. I risked a glance back to the chasm, expecting to see a mess of translucent matter rippling with myriad lights spilling forth, but apart from the black scar of the chasm, there was nothing. Nothing, apart from a sinister schlupping sound that made me want to piss myself.

I ran. Ailsa was a dead weight in my arms, but I didn't stop. Instead, I continued to carry her along the tunnel until it opened up into another large cavern. Rather than enter it alone, I set Ailsa down upon the floor near its entrance. She slumped to one side, her head lolling and eyes dull.

"Ailsa," I said, all the time listening for any telltale slurping sounds that might hint at that thing following us. "Ailsa, wake up. Please, wake up."

I snapped my fingers in front of her face and shook her gently. Finally, she blinked, and whatever had transfixed her fled. She looked around herself, bewildered, until her eyes met mine.

"Lights..." she said.

"I know," I replied.

"I don't know what happened. I saw them in the darkness. Then, they filled everything. It was like I wasn't there, anymore." She shuddered and looked fearfully back up the tunnel.

"I know."

"I don't like this place."

"Neither do I."

"Do you think Brett is safe?"

The question came from out of nowhere, a complete gut-punch. After all we had been through, her mind was still preoccupied by Brett.

"I don't know." I knew I sounded stiff, but I couldn't help it. She glanced up at me, her brows drawn. I tried to smooth my features into something that resembled worry, but the little dawning light in her eyes told me all I needed to know. She clapped me on the shoulder and stood up.

"We should probably just get going,"

I nodded dumbly.

I followed her into the new cavern, my heart in tatters. Back there, on the beach, I could have sworn she...No. I smiled to myself, a self-deprecating and bitter gesture. She didn't. She never had. Even with all the crazy, Brett was the one she held a candle for, and it looked like nothing was going to change that.

I dragged my attention from pathetic self-pity and focused on the new cavern. This one was smaller than the others, and the ever-present bioluminescent algal growths that clung to the walls bathed it in that weird blue-green glow. In a way, I preferred the darkness to this. At least the darkness felt natural, whereas the light the algae produced gave everything a strange, alien quality.

Where the walls were spare of algae, pictograms and hieroglyphs covered them. The nearest one showed all manner of strange creatures kneeling around a monolith, possibly in worship. Upon the monolith were piled the disembodied heads of what I guessed were sacrifices. All around them, the same phrases were copied over and over in a language I didn't have a hope in understanding, but the macabre nature of the scene made me feel uneasy nonetheless.

Together, we moved further into the cavern, taking in the other carvings. I am not kidding when I say Bosch himself wouldn't dare depict the stuff we witnessed upon those walls. It took me a little while to fully comprehend what I was faced with, and even now, I don't think my mind was fully capable of taking in every terrible detail carved into the stone.

Great beasts, mad composites of aquatic creatures and hideous...things visited every single horror I could dream up—and quite a few I couldn't, but I doubt I would ever forget—upon the earth. Where humans did figure, they were always as sacrifice, or on one carved stele I would rather forget, vessels to propagate new monsters. It was not this that frightened me the most, nor what really made me wonder if I'd started to go totally round the twist. No, that dubious honour goes to the fact that no matter how hard I concentrated, no matter how much I squinted and traced the lines with my finger, the images of these monsters would not settle into anything recognizable; instead, they writhed and changed, taking on newer, even more hideous forms until I was forced to look away, my head pounding.

I was so wrapped up in myself that I didn't notice Ailsa staring at the murals, her face a picture of terror.

"What's wrong?" I asked.

She didn't answer me.

"Ailsa," I said. "Ailsa, what's wrong?" I touched her arm, and she jumped as if I'd bitten her.

"I...I've seen these things before," she said, her voice shaking. "When I...when I worked for the geological survey, on Nuarakhu Island in the South Pacific."

Nuarakhu! I knew she'd been on that expedition, and I even knew the basic story of what happened—anyone with access to the research did—but none of the survivors had ever given any details other than there must have been a terrible accident.

Ailsa whispered something under her breath—something unintelligible, full of glottal stops and harsh consonants. I had no idea what she was saying. I made to ask her what she was doing, but my question caught in my throat when I realized she was reading it from the wall.

"It happened quickly," she said, her eyes fixed upon the carvings. "We were excited at having found such a place. We had been told Nuarakhu was uninhabited, and in a way, the experts were right. It was uninhabited by people..."

Chapter Seven

The Nuarakhu Incident

2:00 a.m., 25th February, Four Years Earlier.

The light pierced the darkness, a great bolt of blue and white that crackled down from the heavens. Ailsa rolled over in her sleeping bag and let out a frustrated sigh.

"Not another fucking storm..."

Next to her, Mark snorted in amusement but did not open his eyes.

"I thought this was supposed to be a tropical paradise," she said. "The Bounty adverts lied to me."

"Ahhh, now that's where you went wrong. Y'see, tropical places only *look* like paradise. In reality, they are sweaty, mosquito-bitten hell holes—"

"Yeah, yeah. I know. You've told me before, but still...*more* rain?"

The sky burned again, this time accompanied by a growl of thunder. The air felt fizzy, and all around them, people were stirring, sitting up, and whining to themselves.

More storms meant it was time for everyone to go and collect their precious equipment. They thought it built to last, built to survive such places, but none of them—not ever Doctor Schmidt, with all his years of exploring the most inhospitable places on Earth—had experienced anything quite like this. It was like the island held a very personal grudge against them.

One-by-one, they peeled down their sleeping bags, rooted around for hiking boots, and left the shelter. The sky was full of grumbles, alive with electricity and the metallic taste of incoming rain.

When they had first arrived, Ailsa was the first to unbuckle her seatbelt and jump free; exciting though the ride in a helicopter was, it was nothing compared to the delights she was positive lay before her. Now, she wasn't so sure. Nuarakhu Island, officially classified as uninhabited, made it very attractive to prospectors. She'd signed up to work with the National Geological Survey as soon as she heard the trip was a possibility, figuring that it might scratch her itch for a little bit of genuine adventure rather than being stuck behind a monitor measuring seismic activity in the Pacific.

The sun had been hot on her skin that day, drying the sweat that had accumulated during her flight. Behind her, the team began to unpack their supplies from the belly of the helicopter. There was enough for a two-week stay—more, if they were careful—but this was only a preliminary expedition. A week at most, or so Ailsa had been told. The extra supplies were simply because the weather patterns around the island could be unpredictable, and the lack of decent landing points meant if a storm blew up, they could end up stranded. Rather than worry Ailsa, this excited her even more. For the first time in her scientific life, she was on the cutting edge. Rather than the safe, well-explored outcrops of Hawaii, she finally had the chance to explore somewhere truly remote. The small group of scientists watched as the helicopter shrank to a small, black dot on the horizon and then disappeared.

Now, the real fun could begin—or so she had thought.

A scream ripped through the night. Ailsa's head shot up, her heart racing. What the fuck was that?

Mark grinned.

"Probably just a howler monkey," he said.

"Sounded more like a person," Ailsa said.

Mark stooped down, unhooked the trip wire from his camera, and wound it up in his hands. It did not escape Ailsa's notice that they were shaking.

"They often do. Don't worry, Ails...you'll get used to it."

Ailsa bristled a bit—he never grew tired to reminding her she was the noob—and ripped the camera from its holding.

"Hey! Watch it!" Mark took the camera from her with far gentler hands. "That's worth more than you are...be careful."

A deafening clap of thunder heralded the coming onslaught of the rain, which pattered through the dense foliage.

"Shit. Shit. Here." He thrust the camera at her, again. She stuffed it inside her shirt to protect it from the worst of the rain. Another shriek rose above the cacophony of the storm, and the sweat that ran down Ailsa's back froze.

That was no monkey. Noob or not, she was sure of it. Mark crab walked toward her, his arms full of electrical equipment.

"What're you doing? Come on. Don't just stand there gawking! We need to get this lot back to base. If we don't, it'll be ruined!"

Ailsa glanced into the depths of the virgin jungle and shuddered.

"Just a monkey," she muttered to herself and followed the bobbing light of Mark's flashlight back to camp.

The storm raged all night and half the next morning, confining everyone to base camp. They tried to busy themselves with their various projects—the analysis of camera footage, various insect traps, rock samples and more—but the atmosphere under the canvas was one of sullen frustration. They had come to explore the unexplored, not huddle together under canvas avoiding the rain.

It was Raj, Doctor Schmidt's current Ph.D. student, who first noticed Clive was missing.

At first, they didn't think much of his absence. He was the team's adventurer—their rock climber, navigator, and survival expert. If anyone knew how to look after himself, it was Clive. As the rains eased and the jungle reawoke, the faint stirrings of unease began.

"We'll look for him after we set up the equipment again," Doctor Schmidt said. "I am sure he's fine, though. In fact, I wager he'll probably be waiting for us here by the time we return."

He wasn't. He still hadn't returned by the time they bedded down for the night. He also wasn't there when morning broke or when the team gathered to make breakfast. The unease by now had tightened—not quite into fear, but into that limbo zone just beneath the surface of all their minds.

Where was Clive?

The unspoken question buzzed between them, forcing them to eat in silence. Ailsa, digging into rubbery reconstituted eggs, tried to forget the screams she had heard the night of the storm. Because, Mark said it had been a monkey. A monkey. Nothing more.

They cleared the breakfast things away and drifted off into their work groups.

Ailsa went to join the geology team, but something in the mud just to the left of the tent's entrance caught her eye.

A footprint.

Or was it?

She hunkered down to inspect the imprint. It looked vaguely humanoid in that it had a heel was kind of triangular in shape, but that was where any other similarities stopped. If anything, it looked like a…like a…she struggled to find the words. A flipper? That was closer than a footprint, but still way off. Its toes—if they were toes—jaunted off to the left in a weird angle that made her wince. Maybe it wasn't a footprint after all. Rather like finding pictures in clouds, she was making footprints out of a random collection of perfectly natural depressions in the mud. Yes. That was it. It had to be—

Hang on—was that…?

Another, identical impression in the mud a foot or so away from the first. This was followed by another, and then another—a trackway of depressions that led from their research station, back into the jungle.

A shiver prickled at her back of her neck, and she felt a chill despite the all-pervading heat. Was something watching them?

No. Stop being ridiculous. She mentally slapped herself. Just jumpy due to Clive's apparent disappearance, that's all. Nothing else.

Nothing. Else.

* * * *

Two days later, Clive still hadn't returned. They'd thought about mounting a rescue mission, but the truth was without Clive to guide them, they were pretty much fumbling around in the dark. Then, there were the footprints.

Ailsa decided to keep her discovery to herself, but the following morning their camp was littered with them. Raj and Annie swore blind that they hadn't seen anything, despite being on watch—after Clive's disappearance, no one felt safe enough to sleep anymore—but they had heard a series of weird croaks and whistles in the jungle around them.

She followed Mark more out of habit than any real desire to work. That in itself was strange. She'd fought tooth and nail to be included on this expedition, but now, she was kind of wishing she was still at home enjoying a mocha latte and some particularly terrible daytime TV. What was wrong with her? She rubbed a sweaty hand over her face. Get it together! Daytime TV, indeed…

"Oh, for fucks sake!" Mark rushed forward, snapping a jungle plant back so that it hit her squarely in the face.

"Hey! Watch what you're...doing...what the fuck?"

She raced after him, all thoughts of recrimination gone. Their site—the bores, the little generator they were using, even their little microscope that lay in pieces, smashed beyond all recognition.

"How did this happen?" Mark ran both his hands over his bald head, a sure sign of stress. Ailsa just shook her head dumbly.

"There's nothing left. Everything is just...just...how did this happen?"

That really was the question. It was widely believed Nuarakhu couldn't support life any larger than a gibbon, and there were no indigenous people...or so they thought. Whatever had destroyed their site was not only larger than a gibbon, it knew how to operate a screwdriver. Well, kind of. This wasn't just something large smashing its way through the jungle. This level of destruction told them something was deliberately pulling things apart. The fact that the screws had been taken out of the camera housing told them that much. Uneasy thoughts of weird-shaped footprints popped into Ailsa's mind.

"Maybe, we should just pick up and go through what we do have?" she said.

Mark grumbled under his breath but nodded in agreement. "Yeah. Makes sense. Even so..."

"I know. Frustrating."

"Frustrating? Fucking blood-boiling is more like. Just what the hell is going on around here?"

They gathered up what was left of the equipment in silence. Beside the smashed remains, they found bits of stone and shell scattered on the ground, and she realized that whoever—or whatever—had tried to take apart the equipment hadn't been so random as they first thought. It was just that the tools they'd used weren't the right ones for the job.

If Mark noticed, he didn't say anything, but Ailsa did notice him picking up a few shell fragments and frowning. When they were finished, Ailsa was only too pleased to leave.

* * * *

"You too, huh?"

Raj was waiting for them outside the main research tent, trying to piece together a broken video camera. He hissed between his teeth and threw the bits on the floor.

"Everything was smashed. Doctor Schmidt couldn't believe it. He's furious."

"He's not the only one," Mark muttered.

"Does he have any idea what might be happening?" Ailsa asked.

Raj shook his head.

"He's not sure, but he's trying to glean as much as he can from the smashed cameras. He's got Annie on to it—hopefully, she might be able to piece something together."

"I can't believe this," Mark said. "We were told this place was uninhabited."

"Allegedly, it is," Raj said. "There's no evidence of any tribal activity—"

"No evidence?" Mark held up a broken camera. "Then, what did this?"

Raj raised his hands in from of him and shrugged.

"Hey, don't shoot the messenger. Look on the bright side. Maybe, there is something new here. Technology's loss could be cryptozoology's gain."

Mark rolled his eyes, but curiosity prickled at Ailsa. Maybe, Raj was right.

Later that afternoon, Doctor Schmidt called a full meeting. Every department was in the same situation. Every single piece of equipment was now smashed beyond repair, and without any real means of fixing it, was there really any point in staying? The groups murmured amongst themselves, some in agreement, some in dissent, and a good deal in fear. Clive's disappearance weighed heavily upon all of them, and it had become something of an elephant in the room. Everyone knew it happened, but no one really wanted to talk about it.

From the corner of the room, Annie spoke up. "Uh, boss...I think you'd better come and look at this."

Doctor Schmidt gave her an irritated glance.

"Can't it wait?"

"No, I don't think it can." Her eyes, glued to the monitor in front of her, filled with a creeping horror.

Raj stood up and wandered over to peer over her shoulder. He watched for a moment. His hand flew to his mouth, and all the color drained from his face.

"Holy sh...Annie's right, Doctor Schmidt. You need to see this."

Doctor Schmidt let out a frustrated sigh and sat next to Annie. One-by-one, the rest of the expedition crowded around Annie's laptop. She fiddled with a piece of equipment, and a small square in the center of the screen crackled to life.

At first, there was nothing but static. After a few, breathless seconds, flashes of coherent film flickered before them. The jungle, eerie in shades of black and green, was empty. The date and time ticked over in the corner. Then, back to static. To the jungle. To static. Jungle. Static.

To a face.

The whole group recoiled. The image had only flashed up for a fraction of a second, but the effect on them was electric.

"What the hell was that?" someone whispered.

Annie paused the tape.

"I don't know." She turned and gave them all an ominous look. "Keep watching."

Ailsa swallowed hard. She glanced over at Mark. He was riveted to the screen.

Static. Jungle. Static.

Clive.

All hell broke loose.

"Clive!"

"What the—"

"What is he doing?"

"C-Clive?"

"What's wrong with him?" Ailsa said.

Annie paused the tape again, focusing on Clive's face. His eyes were blank, with something black smudged across his temples. It didn't take them long to figure out it was blood. Blood probably from the wound where his right ear had once been.

"Who...what...what's happened to him?" Hideki, one of the botanists, asked.

"Why the hell is he smashing up our equipment?" Mark said.

"I don't think he is," Annie said. "Keep watching."

Ailsa found herself unwilling to do that. The memory of the footprints kept swimming up from the murk of her mind. The footprints and the shells.

Clive was back. The recording flickered and jumped,

forbidding them from focusing too long on anything. After a while, it became apparent Clive wasn't just standing there. He was speaking.

"W-what's he saying?"

"Don't know. Can't work it out."

All heads craned forward.

"It looks like...looks like he's repeating the same thing, over and over again."

"'Save yourselves'" Marlon, one of the biologists, said.

"What?"

"Save yourselves." He gave them all a sheepish look. "My brother is deaf."

"Save yourselves?" Doctor Schmidt said. "What does he mean by that?"

"Keep watching," said Annie. She unpaused the recording, and the little square moved again. Clive continued his silent entreaty, to the point where Ailsa wondered if it was skipping.

It wasn't. Behind him, just out of focus, something moved. It crept up behind Clive, who glanced fearfully over his shoulder. He brought both his hands up to his face, and screamed. Ailsa didn't need sound to hear his terror. She could see it in every line on his face.

The recording ended.

No one spoke.

No one breathed.

Then, they all panicked together. A babbling cacophony of unnamed fear surged up and burst, shattering the brief silence.

"Okay, everyone. I said, okay!" Doctor Schmidt held up a placatory hand. "I'll call Rescue. We need to leave as soon as possible."

"What about Clive?"

"We'll inform Rescue. They're trained for this kind of thing."

Ailsa barely heard the rest of the conversation. That final frame of Clive's terrified face lodged in her mind, refusing to move.

All departments packed what remained of their equipment quickly. A fearful hush had fallen over the camp—something that unnerved Ailsa even more than the babbling panic. She wasn't used to this. Usually, the atmosphere between different departments was one of good-natured rivalry, and for them to be quietly cooperating...it wasn't right. It just wasn't right.

They struck their tents and gathered outside the main shelter, where Schmidt was swearing at the Sat phone.

"Oh, for God's sake! Work! What is wrong with you?"

No one dared to answer him.

"It's no good. The atmospherics here are terrible. Maybe, if we hike back to the beach, we'll get better reception."

They all gave the jungle that surrounded them a surreptitious look. Again, they all thought it, but no one was willing to say it. They'd managed to find their base camp under the expert guidance of Clive, but Clive was no longer with them. The unspoken question hung over them. Exactly how were they going to find the beach?

"It's this way," Hideki said, hoisting his backpack onto one shoulder.

From the way the rest of the team exchanged glances, Ailsa wasn't so sure.

* * * *

"I thought you said you knew where you were going?"

"No, I just said I thought it was this way—"

"Oh, great. So, we're lost?"

"I never said that!"

"So, where are we?"

"I don't know—"

"What do you mean, 'I don't know'?"

"Oh, for Christ sake. Would you lay off him? He's doing his best."

"Oh! Well that's fine, then. As long as he's doing his best."

"Yeah, doing his best is going to get us killed!"

"Just stop it, everyone! We'll find the beach. It wasn't that far away."

"Not that far away? It took us all *day* to find it!"

Ailsa clutched her head and tried to use the padded straps of her backpack to stop her ears. It didn't work, but she was getting desperate. Anything to block out the constant bickering.

They weren't lost. How could they be lost? It had all started out so well. The path that Clive had cut from the beach to their site had been pretty wide and easy to follow. He even put slash marks into the trunks of the trees, so they could follow them if need be. She glanced around. No slash marks. Where had the slash marks gone? She was sure she'd seen one not too long ago. She took a peek at her watch. It had stopped. Typical. Their compasses were also less than useful. According to them, they'd been heading in a steady northwest direction all day. If that was true, why were they still in thick jungle? Where was the beach? It hadn't taken them this long to get to the site, after all.

"I'm sure we've passed this tree before," Mark said. Ailsa couldn't help but agree. It was huge, and according to Terry, their tree expert, probably a species new to science. It was kind of hard not to recognize it. "Look. Look. Stop. Everyone, just stop. This is madness. We're going around in circles."

"No, we aren't," Doctor Schmidt said. "This is the way. I am sure. The compass says we are still heading northwest. And can't you hear the surf?"

They all stopped and listened. Sure enough, above the chirruping of the jungle, they could hear the boom and roar of the sea.

"He's right!"

"It could still be miles away."

"No, it's closer than that."

"The wind is in the right direction. It could make it seem closer than it is."

"Why must you always be so fucking pessimistic?"

"Because we're going the wrong way!" Mark's voice rose above the others, and they all fell silent once again. "Come on, Ernst. Time for a different plan. If we keep going like this, we're going to get lost. Well, more lost, anyway—"

"No we aren't!" There was a bite to Doctor Schmidt's voice that Ailsa had never heard before. She stole a glance his way. His glasses were steamed, and there was a disheveled wildness to him that was totally at odds with his usually calm and neat demeanor. If she didn't know better, she'd say he was on the verge of panic...

Mark squared up to Schmidt and stuck his jaw out.

"So, you think we're okay?"

"I don't think it, Doctor Galloway. I know it."

"Oh, right? And how do you know that?"

"Because we're heading toward the beach." Schmidt spoke in the slow, deliberate way usually reserved for the very young and the very stupid. "If a sound gets louder, you're generally heading in the right direction."

"The sound isn't getting louder, you knob. It's staying the same, because we're fucking lost!"

"No need for profanities, Doctor Galloway. You know I do not like such language."

"I don't give a flying *fuck* whether you like my fucking language, Schmidt. I'm more concerned about you getting us fucking killed!"

"Why must you persist in this fantasy that we're all going to get killed, Doctor Galloway?"

"Seriously? The video, Ernst—the fucking video. Clive. You saw it! You saw him! Something did that to him, and I'm not about to hang around here waiting for whatever it is to find me."

"Well, it's good that we're not hanging around, isn't it? All we need to do is keep going. The beach is not far away—"

Mark lost it.

"The beach is far away, because we're going the wrong fucking way!" He balled his fists up, and for a moment, Ailsa wondered if he would punch Schmidt. Instead, he took a deep breath and steadied himself. "Okay. Fine. Fine. You go your way. I'll go mine." He turned to address the rest of the group. "Anyone coming?"

No one stepped up.

"Anyone? Ailsa?"

Ailsa cringed a little, and an uncomfortable, gnawing sensation settled in her stomach. As much as she liked Mark, he wasn't exactly the most...even of people she knew. Schmidt was right—they could hear the beach. As long as they followed the sound, they would be all right. Wouldn't they?

"Well?"

"Maybe, it's just better if we all stay together," Ailsa said. "Clive..."

The look on Mark's face—first hurt surprise, then stubborn anger, made her want to crawl into a hole.

"Right. Like that, is it? Fine. I'll come look for you when you're all ready to admit you're lost."

"Mark!"

"Mate, come on."

"Don't be like that."

"Mark...please..."

He wouldn't listen. He stamped off into the jungle, taking his wounded pride with him.

"Don't worry. He will return," Schmidt said. "If he doesn't, we will inform Rescue that one of our team is still here. For now, we have to move. It'll be dark soon, and I want to find the beach before then."

* * * *

She should have gone with him. She shouldn't have let him go. Should have gone with him. Shouldn't let him go. The thoughts chased themselves around Ailsa's mind until she screwed her eyes up and balled her fists, willing for them to stop, but that just let in the sounds of the jungle—the whirring, the ticking, the chuff-chuff-chuffing of something unseen in the undergrowth. She should have gone with him. Shouldn't have let him go. Gone with him. Let him go. Gone. Go. Maybe, this was how it felt when you went totally nuts. When that little voice in your head just wouldn't shut the fuck up...

They'd been walking for hours. Dusk had settled over them like a shroud, and it wouldn't be long before night blanketed the island. A few of the group were already courting paranoia, convinced that something was watching them, following them, hunting them. Ailsa tried as much as she could to stay out of their way, but that inevitably meant straying closer to Schmidt.

Ailsa's personal experience of a complete mental breakdown was limited to the melodramatic glamorizations of it on TV, but even she could see that Schmidt was losing it. He muttered constantly to himself in German and stalked through the jungle like it had kicked his grandmother in the face, slashing at undergrowth and wantonly ripping up handfuls of plants whenever he could. He kept taking random sharp turns every so often, which meant even if they hadn't been lost before, they were now.

Annie followed him, the Sat phone cradled in her hands. Every now and again, she'd pause to see if she could pick up a signal, any signal, even a whisper of a signal that she might use to get then home, but it was no use. Then, she'd have to run to catch up with them again, because Schmidt refused to stop for anything.

It took a scream to change that.

Hideki gasped out something in Japanese, and the rest of them froze. Behind Ailsa, someone started muttering the Lord's Prayer over and over again.

"Just a gibbon." Another shriek of very human agony silenced Doctor Schmidt.

"Sorry, boss, but that ain't no gibbon..."

Ailsa found herself nodding. That certainly wasn't a gibbon.

Gibbons didn't yell out "God, help me!" for a start.

"Right. We need to...to...Ernst?" Hideki said. He gave the jungle little panicked glances.

"We need to carry on," Schmidt said.

Again, the group erupted.

"No—we need to try to rescue Mark!"

"Are you insane? We need to get out of here!"

"We can't leave him. He needs our help."

"Exactly how are we supposed to do that?"

"We can't leave him!"

"We have to help—"

"For fuck's sake—how?"

"We're never going to get out of here..."

A deep, low rumble took up a rhythm, giving the island a heartbeat.

Drums.

"Oh, dear Lord. Oh, fuck. Oh, Hell—"

"Shut. Up!" Doctor Schmidt barked.

Above them, the stars winked in beat with the drums.

"We need to keep going," Raj said, his voice barely above a whisper. "Away from the...from the..." he trailed off, unable to say the final word. Ailsa understood why. Saying the final word made it true. Saying they were drums made them drums, and that begged the question—what the hell was playing them?

* * * *

Night—real night, not the sodium-lit parody of night that people pretended was real—is black. Really black. So black, you can't see your hand in front of your face, let alone what your feet are doing. They had flashlights, but even their high-powered beams seemed pathetic in the suffocating darkness.

The drums continued to rumble all around them. So did the screams. Out of sheer desperation, Ailsa fished out her emergency earplugs, but even they did nothing to muffle the sound. The drums were part of the island, their noise as much felt as heard.

No matter what they did, no matter what direction they took, the drums grew louder. Doctor Schmidt's muttering grew with it. Georgia was crying. Marlon said the Lord's Prayer on an irritating loop. Most of the others tramped on, their arms wrapped around themselves, each in their own personal worlds of terror.

Ailsa was now sure someone was following them. She shivered and bit back a sob. What had started out as an adventure of a lifetime descended into a hellish nightmare. Something rustled in the undergrowth. She spun around and bumped into Raj, who let out a strangled yelp.

The drums still rolled on.

Doctor Schmidt slashed at the jungle, creating his own path. It was only when the swoosh of his knife stilled that they realized that he too was gone.

Raj ran forward. Ailsa stumbled back. Her feet caught on a log, sending her crashing to the ground. Her flashlight jolted, sputtered and then died, plunging her into darkness. A pair of hands clutched at her. She shrieked and clawed at them before she realized it was Hideki.

The jungle broke out into a cacophony of clicks and croaks, and everything went black.

* * * *

The drums reached fever pitch. Moans and screams joined them, coming from every part of the island. Ailsa and Hideki crouched in stupid terror at the heart of a thicket, as still as stone. Next to them, Annie clutched at the Sat phone, her mouth working at a silent prayer.

Ailsa couldn't make out what the things were. They were bipedal and vaguely humanoid in shape, but beyond that, all comparisons to humanity ended. Whatever they were, they'd brought the group down with efficient ease, grabbing at them one-by-one and dragging them away into the darkness of the jungle. Flashlights pulsated, illuminating a leg here, a flailing limb there, a strange, almost piscine head, a blood soaked face.

She buried her head in her hands and tried to block out the screeches, the moans, the sickening crack of what she could only guess was bone. Hideki tightened his grip upon her, and she bit her bottom lip to stop herself from yelping.

Then, it stopped.

The three of them remained frozen. Was it really over, or were they trying to lull them into a false sense of security to flush them out? The seconds ticked by until they formed unbearable minutes. The normal whirrings of the jungle reasserted themselves, but they remained still. Annie was the first to move. She placed the Sat phone on the floor and scanned for a signal. She was crying now. Huge, silent sobs racked her body and made her clumsy.

Still nothing.

"We're all going to die," Hideki whispered, and then muttered something in Japanese under his breath.

The drums started up, again.

Annie jumped and let out a whimper. Hideki giggled.

"We're all going to die..."

Ailsa regarded him numbly. Usually, she would have told him to shut up, to stop being so stupid. Now, he seemed to be talking perfect sense.

As predicted, more screams followed the drums. They were further away, but that did little to dull their horror. This time, there were many—their voices all brought together in one perfect, terrible harmony.

"What are they doing to them?" Annie whispered.

Hideki giggled, again. Ailsa screwed her eyes up and shuddered.

"I don't know."

"Shouldn't we at least try to help them?"

"I don't know."

Hideki cackled.

"Too late, now. Look." He then lapsed back into Japanese.

The two women looked to where he pointed. They weren't so far from the beach after all. Through the trees, they could see the flickering light of flaming brands, and under those brands, hopping monstrosities. One turned toward them, and for a heart-stopping moment, Ailsa thought it could see her. She could certainly see it.

Its face resembled something trawled up from the deep-sea, with pinprick eyes and overly large, needle-like teeth. A ridge of spines rose up over its flattened head, like a cock's comb. It grasped its brand with spidery fingers that were connected by membranous webbing, and its skin was covered in an array of oily scales.

"What the hell..." Ailsa breathed. She felt Annie recoil beside her. Hideki snorted and stumbled forward. The creature let out a rumbling croak, and the horde stopped.

"Hideki...Hideki, no!" Annie hissed, but it was too late. Hideki ran in blind panic, crashing through the undergrowth with the fish-creatures following. Ailsa and Annie clung to each other as they ran past, chasing Hideki like a pack of dogs hunts a fox. They caught him quickly, and he wriggled and screeched. The creatures hoisted him high into the air and carried him, almost ceremoniously, down to the beach and off toward the sea.

The beach was now empty, and silence reigned again.

"What the hell is going on? What the fuck are those things?" Annie whispered.

"I don't know, but we can't stay here."

"So, where do we go?"

Ailsa ran both her hands over her face. Why was she the one who had to think up all the answers?

"I don't know!"

"Maybe, we should follow them? Just in case we can...you know...rescue anyone?"

Ailsa didn't even dignify that with an answer. She stared at Annie, and both of them knew the truth.

There was no point in following the others, because the others were dead.

* * * *

The rest of the night passed with a continuing barrage of shrieks and drums. Whatever going on in the shallows, Ailsa and Annie didn't want to know. The nightmare only ended when the pink strips of dawn gashed the night sky. It took until the sun was fully up for them to leave their flimsy sanctuary. Annie tried the Sat phone another time and sobbed when she finally managed to get a message through. The reply was garbled, but held a note of promise—the words "wait", "help" and "beach".

It took them a long time to pluck up the courage to head there. Visions of what they might find swam through their minds, faltering their steps and sapping at their resolve. It was ridiculous. Their only means of escape was from the beach, and surely, nothing could be as bad as the things their imagination could conjure up...

They broke the tree line cautiously. Those strange footprints littered the sand. Just a little way from them, near a collection of rocks that made the headland, stood an array of six-foot poles. Each had something fluttering from them. At first, Ailsa thought they might be flags or banners, and they were, after a fashion. It was only after she recognized Georgia's rather spectacular collection of tattoos did she realize what had actually happened to the rest of the research party.

It was too much for Annie, who threw up in the nearest rock pool. Ailsa surprised herself. She thought she would be joining her, but instead, she felt a numb detachment from the whole situation.

That, and she couldn't help but wonder what had happened to those whose skins weren't on display.

Chapter Eight

"Then, what happened?"

Even though it seemed cruel, I had to know. Ailsa stared blankly at a point around a foot or so above my left shoulder.

"We waited. A few hours later, the helicopter came to pick us up."

"What about the rest of the research party?"

"Official records state there was a tragic accident. They didn't find anything apart from the skins. They swore Annie and me to secrecy. Annie couldn't cope, and they carted her off to the nuthouse shortly afterward. She's still there, as far as I know."

"And...and how about you?"

"Me? I threw myself into my studies. Made a name for myself. That's the good thing about being sworn to secrecy. No one else knows, so I could apply for other jobs, get involved in other research projects. Nuarakhu comes up in conversation from time-to-time, but since there are really no official records of the expedition anymore, it's pretty easy to play dumb."

"What happens if someone decides to go back to Nuarakhu?"

"Won't happen. As far as I know, the military nuked the place about a month later."

"They...nuked it? Isn't that a bit extreme?"

"If you'd been there, you wouldn't think so," Ailsa said. "They depth-charged the reef and carpet-bombed the actual island. I only know the barest of details. They said it was for my own peace of mind."

I thought of the sudden shift in the seabed that had triggered our expedition and wondered what else might have been nuked recently, but no. We'd know if something like that had happened on such a scale to cause such a huge movement in the Earth's crust...wouldn't we?

We sat in silence for a moment longer. I didn't once doubt the truth of Ailsa's tale. The look of haunted terror in her eyes told me everything I needed to know. I glanced back up at the murals and was grateful we hadn't come across those... things, yet. Then, I thought of the weird croaks we'd heard in the algal forest, and the footprints that seemed to match Ailsa's description.

"They're here, aren't they?" I asked.

Ailsa closed her eyes and nodded. Funny. I never knew there was an emotion beyond dread. I knew something had rattled her before, that our hiding had been beyond mere caution. Maybe, it was my fault. Maybe, I should have made more of a deal of it all, asked her more questions, made her give me proper answers

"I didn't say anything before...I didn't want to face the reality that they were real, let alone here. I'm sorry, Tom. I'm so sorry. I should have told you before. I should have—"

"Shhh. There's no point in beating yourself up about it. I don't think you telling me about Nuarakhu any earlier would have changed any of this."

She gave me a weak smile.

"Thanks."

"You're welcome."

"So...what do we do, now?"

It was the question I was dreading.

"I don't know."

Admitting this pained me, but what else could I say? If anything, she was the expert here. She'd been in this kind of situation before. Me? The most dangerous situation I'd ever been in was when we screwed up the kind of work permit we needed to operate equipment off the coast of Cuba. The only reason I was involved in this mess was because I discovered the anomaly on the sea floor. To me, this expedition meant nothing more than an interesting quirk in the Earth's natural cycle. Too late, I found out it was anything but natural.

"We can't stay here," she said.

"No, we can't," I said.

"We have to find Brett."

Brett, again. I suppose that was the one thing keeping her going. Me too, if I was forced to admit it. Find Brett. It seemed infinitely more achievable than "find a way home".

I gave the carvings one last look of distaste and stood up. Ailsa wouldn't even afford them that much respect. She just shivered and followed my lead wordlessly. I'd never seen her so withdrawn, and part of me regretted asking her anything about Nuarakhu, but it had been done. All we could do was move on now.

At the end of the cavern was another archway, but this wasn't like the others. This one didn't have a door embedded into it, nor did it lead to another nightmarish cavern. Instead, its entrance looked as if covered by a film of black oil, which rippled in the glow of the bioluminescent algae.

We both peered at it, but the darkness was absolute. Ailsa glanced at me, and I shrugged. I had no idea what it was, either. I picked up a stone and tested its weight in my hand.

"Are you sure that's a good idea?" Ailsa asked, biting her fingernails. Usually, they were manicured to the point of obsession. I'd noticed, because geologist's fingernails are usually ragged stumps filled with grit. Now, she'd bit hers to the quick, and in some places, until they bled. I decided not to make an issue of it, even though it worried me. We all deal with stressful situations in different ways. Shame, my usual go-to method—run and hide until it all blows over—was pretty useless right now.

"What else can we do?" I said. "This is it—the end of the road. There is nowhere left to go. We either stay in this cavern and rot, or we try to find out what is on the other side of that archway."

"If there *is* anything. There could be nothing. There should be nothing. I mean, come on...it's almost cliché. An archway with a weird, shimmery covering? Wasn't there a film way back about this?"

She was right. I'd seen enough science fiction nonsense over the years to realize this was one big, cliché-ridden joke, or it would have been if it hadn't been real. A chuckle bubbled up inside me. At least, that's what I wanted it to be. If it *was* a giggle, then I'd start to seriously worry about my sanity, because real men don't giggle. I bit it back and nodded, instead.

I wound back my arm as if I was pitching a baseball and threw the stone at the opening, half hoping it would bounce back, half hoping it wouldn't. The stone sailed through the oil. Its passage left little, concentric ripples, as if I had thrown it into a still pond.

I didn't hear it clatter to the ground on the other side.

"Okay, so things can go through it," Ailsa said. "What now?"

I bit the inside of my cheek. If we'd had a camera, I would've attached it to a pole—also something we lacked—with something. What that something might be, I also don't know. Seaweed? Then, I would record what was on the other side. Since we didn't have a camera, or a pole, or any means of attaching the two together, that idea was scuppered. I tasted blood and ran my tongue along the inside of my cheek. It felt spongy and pitted. I really had to stop doing that.

"Okay. Okay. So, we can't stay here. That we already know. Quite honestly, I have no idea if we're going to get out of this alive."

"Tom!" Ailsa's sharp intake of breath spoke of true shock. I had voiced the unvoiceable, at last.

"Well, do you?"

Ailsa paused.

"No, but..."

"But what?"

"I thought the same on Nuarakhu, and I'm still here."

"You had at least the glimmer of hope there. No matter what happened, the helicopter was going to return at some point. Take a look around. Any Sat phone here? Does the coastguard know where we are? The Navy Seals? No. No one knows, Ailsa. *No* one." For some reason, I found myself getting more and more annoyed with each word. "We're stuck here, and the way I see it, we can either die here and now, or die trying to get out. I don't know about you, but I'm not all that keen on just sitting here and waiting for death."

"Tom...please. You don't have to shout. Please, Tom. Don't shout."

I dropped my arms. I hadn't even noticed I was waving them around. This place was getting to me and not in a good way. I thought of Brett, and the maniacal glint in his eyes. Did I have them, now? Was I finally following Brett down that path?

"I'm sorry, Ails." I stepped toward her. She shrank back, just a little, but enough for me to know I'd unsettled her. "I really am. Sorry. Come on."

I held my hand out to her. She eyed it for a second longer than I would have liked, and then took it, allowing me to wrap my other arm around her.

"I can't promise I'll get you out of this alive," I said. "I can promise I'll give it a damn good try."

"Okay, then." She looked over at the strange portal. "We'll do what we have to do."

I swallowed. Hard. Bravado is a fine thing right up until you're actually challenged. Then, it scuttles off, leaving you feeling like a prize prick, and an absolutely terrified prize prick at that. I licked my lips. They felt leathery and tasted of salt and blood.

"Right. Okay. The archway. Okay."

She looked up at me again, and I thought I saw something in her eyes that might get within the ballpark of respect, maybe even affection. So, that's what you had to do to get the girl, was it? Risk your life—and hers—by offering to prod something unnamable and unknowable. The giggle raised its ugly head, again. If only I'd known about that in college...

I reached forward and paused, my fingertips hovering an inch from the surface of the oil. Again, out of habit, I bit the inside of my cheek and felt something squishy sheer off. This time, the giggle burst out of me, making me snort. What that fuck was I doing? My fingers edged closer. What the fuck was this thing? Closer. What the fuck would happen next?

I closed my eyes. The throbbing of my heart made my head ache. I took in a deep breath, held it, and drove my hand into the miasma. It felt cold, but that was all. I wrenched my hand back.

Nothing. No injury. No withering. No evidence whatsoever of anything wrong. Just my hand, grubby but still intact.

"Looks like it's okay," Ailsa said. The look she gave me now shifted from potential respect to one of worry. Worry? She wasn't the one risking her balls here. She was just standing there, watching and doing nothing.

"Did you hear that?"

I paused mid-mind rant. All I could hear was the distant drip of water and nothing else.

No...not nothing else. Something else. Something new. The soft slap of skin against a wet floor. Then, a deep, growling croak followed by an answering hiss.

"Oh, shit!" My voice dropped to a hiss. Ailsa, panic drawn in every line of her body, leapt up and scuttled around, looking for a place to hide.

"The archway!" I said.

"No no no no. What if they go through it? What if they follow us? No, we have to hide...hide...somewhere, hide..." She was off.

I cursed under my breath and ran after her, keeping my body low. A strange jibber filled the air. An icy shudder ran the length of my spine. Images of strange composites ran through my head as I tried to piece together the creatures from Ailsa's description. Up ahead, shadows flickered against the cavern's ceiling, twisting the hopping forms that created them into even more grotesque forms. The stench of abyssal sludge and rot wafted toward me. They were close, much closer than I had anticipated.

Were they hunting us?

Where was Ailsa?

I couldn't speak. Not that I wanted to. I didn't want those things to find me, but it was more than that. A fist of panic squeezed my throat, making even breathing difficult. I hunkered down, trying to make myself as small as possible, and shuffled backward, behind one of the carved stele.

Something seized my ankle.

Sheer instinct stopped me from screaming out.

"Under here!" Ailsa hissed and pulled me back. She'd found a small gap under what looked like a large, stone bench—just big enough for the two of us to squeeze under. I fell to my belly, my heart clanging in my ears, and I wriggled forward. I barely had time to haul my feet under me when Ailsa froze.

I could only see their feet. Or should I say, flippers. They were a mottled, greenish-gray with long, spindly, and webbed toes. Their stench was incredible. They croaked at one another in a parody of language and then moved closer to the archway.

I held my breath, but they didn't go through. Instead, they milled around its entrance as if searching for something. A heated exchange followed. The largest of the creatures jabbed at another with its spear, and the smaller one hopped away. I didn't need to understand the language to know that one had been sent off on an errand of some sort. The remaining creatures—there were four of them—moved away from the archway, back toward the antechamber.

I felt a sharp nudge in the small of my back.

We need to go through, Ailsa mouthed at me.

I shook my head. Was she insane? What if those things followed us?

We can't stay here.

On cue, my neck cricked painfully as I tried to crane my head up and spy where the creatures had actually gone.

They might follow us, I mouthed.

She shrugged. She was right.

What choice did we have?

I gave her a small, jerky nod and held my hand up, a sign for her to stay where she was. It took everything I had to slide myself out from underneath that bench, just enough so I could see if the coast was clear. The creatures were nearby. I could hear them, but by some miracle, they weren't in sight of the archway. Maybe, they weren't hunting us. Maybe, they didn't know we were here. Maybe...

Ailsa darted past me and dove headlong into the oil.

I gasped out her name. A croak from the other room answered me. Now, I knew I had no choice. Whether they had heard me or not didn't matter. The surface of the portal quivered.

I crawled through.

Chapter Nine

Have you ever stood out in the snow in your underwear at 3:00 AM? Neither have I, but compared to the cold of that portal, I imagine that would feel positively tropical. I had my suspicions as to the nature of that archway before I crawled through it—that it was some kind of gateway, or if you would forgive my whimsy, a dimensional portal—but I wasn't expecting it to be quite so cold. I nearly collapsed on the other side. It felt like an age before my frozen lungs would allow me to draw breath and even longer before my teeth stopped chattering. Ice crystals peppered my hair, and after an investigation with my little finger, I pulled more from my nostrils.

"A-Ails-s-s-a," I hissed.

A lump a little way from me stirred.

"Fuck," it said.

I scrabbled toward her. She clung to me like I was the last good thing on this earth, and you never know. Maybe, I was. I dusted the ice crystals out of her hair, and together, we backed away from the portal. You never knew what might be following.

I had my eyes firmly on the archway, but Ailsa's attention was obviously elsewhere. I felt her tense beside me.

"Where the hell are we?"

"Is that really important? We need to get...away..." I turned around, and the world swooped around me. We were at the center of a massive amphitheatre. Stretching out in all directions where line after line of huge, pointed crystals. They all glowed green, each with a small, red heart, and there had to be thousands of them.

What really made my heart stop wasn't the crystals, though. It was what stood between them. Humanoid figures, each a hideous mixture of man and fish. Statues. Statues of the...things.

Ailsa's hand flew to her mouth. She scuttled backward. I didn't have to ask her what these things were. I already knew. I'd seen enough of them before, just not close up. These were the things from Nuarakhu. The things carved into the rock of the antechamber that led here.

These were the things that ran this place.

I took a step toward one. Their construction really was quite exquisite. They had even managed to find a stone that allowed them to depict their mottled skin correctly. I reached up to touch one. They had to stand at nearly eight feet tall, and they were so life like, so real…

The statue quivered, and a droplet of a viscous liquid rolled down a huge, translucent fang.

I froze. These weren't statues.

"Oh, dear Lord…"

"What is it?" Ailsa asked.

"They're real. They aren't statues. They're…the creatures. The things—"

"What?" There was no mistaking the horrified disbelief in her voice.

"It's okay, I think," I said. "They're in some kind of torpid state." I reached up and dared to touch the thing's skin. It felt rubbery and ice cold. "Think about it. Many deep-sea creatures enter such states when food is scarce. Maybe, this is something similar—"

"You mean, they're waiting for food?"

"No, no…I don't think that's it. I think they're waiting for something."

"Waiting for what?"

"Beats me."

A strange, clicking sound distracted me. It wasn't quite in rhythm, and as it grew steadily louder, it bothered me. I stepped away from the creature, trying to find its source. It seemed to be coming from the dais…from the floor. I crept back to the archway, listening hard. Then, it hit me.

It was underneath me.

I looked down. An array of strange, concentric circles lay there, all interlinked. I knelt down to touch one of the rings. They felt greasy, and were made of a strange, purplish mineral. I jumped back up when one slid a quarter of an inch to my right. I realized it wasn't just for decoration.

It was some sort of clock.

I looked up. The ceiling was at least 100 feet above us and made of glass. There were strange runes carved upon its surface in what I assumed might be lead, but who knew in this place? Across the middle, nine massive crystals—diamonds?—also inlaid, like a superimposed galaxy across the night sky.

No...wait. Not like a galaxy. They *were* a galaxy. I strained my eyes to see past the decorative ceiling. Beyond that, a starscape with no constellations I recognized spread out. One of the crystals was glowing red. It matched one of the stars. An uneasy feeling churned my guts. What was it Brett had said? About the stars being right?

"Tom..." There was an urgent note of anxiety in Ailsa's voice. "I think you need to come and look at this."

I tore my eyes from the unfamiliar stars. She was standing in front of one of the crystals. It had to be seven or eight feet tall and at least three feet wide. She was staring into its depths, mesmerized by something.

Her eyes flicked to mine, and I saw fear buried deep.

"Just take a look."

She shuffled out of my way, disgust curling her lip. I frowned. What could be that bad? Then, I remembered where I was. Oh, yes—it could be that bad.

I craned forward and peered into the depths of the crystal. At first, I couldn't make out what it was that lay at its center. I followed a line here, a crack there, until my mind began to piece it all together.

I took an involuntary step backward.

"Hell, no."

Ailsa just nodded.

"People?"

"People."

"How? Wh-where...why?"

Ailsa shook her head, her eyes like saucers.

"They're being prepared, you know. Prepared for Their arrival. It's soon. See the stars? They're almost right. Almost, but not quite."

I jumped, and a barking shriek escaped me. Ailsa simply screamed.

Brett stood up from behind one of the crystals. He caressed its surface, a covetous smile playing along his lips.

"Brett!" At last, I gathered enough of my wits to speak. "What the fuck are you doing here?"

He continued to stroke the crystal.

"She's here."

"Who's here?" I suddenly felt very angry. What the hell was he playing at? Who was here? Idiot! "What the hell are you talking about?"

"She is. My sister. Marissa. She's here. In there." He faced the crystal and laid his cheek against its cool surface.

Now, I knew he'd lost it. Now, the stuff in his wallet made sense. Yes, his sister had disappeared, but she'd died. Drowned, or so I'd heard. How could she be here? It was mental. It was beyond mental. Then I thought of everything we had been through. Suddenly, Brett's assertion didn't feel quite so insane after all.

"Brett," Ailsa said in a soft voice. "We came to find you."

Brett laughed.

"Why did you do that? You have no reason to be here."

"You do?" I said.

"Of course I do." He raised his cheek from the crystal. "I have to help her. Help her break free. Help her fulfill her destiny."

"Fulfill her...Brett, this needs to stop. Just stop this crap. All of it." Again, that anger born of sheer terror surged through me. It was all I could do to stop myself from charging at him, grabbing him by the scruff of his insane neck, and hauling his ass from that damn crystal.

"Stop the what?" I expected him to return to my anger. Instead, he sounded amused. "You think this is crap, do you? I know that's what you all thought, back at the university, but it isn't crap. Neither is it nonsense, insanity, or just plain batshit crazy. It's real. You've looked into one of the crystals. You know what lies at their hearts. They took them, all those years ago...took them, because they needed them. Their numbers have dwindled, and our world has become uncomfortable for Them. They need new hosts—hosts that can withstand what we have done to our world—and now, they have them. All of them. The Lost were never really Lost. They were just...misappropriated. Now, the time has come for Them to return."

Behind me, the concentric rings shifted again, and something unseen clunked into place. Another red light flared to life on the crystalline ceiling. Another star lined up.

Out of the corner of my eye, I saw Brett raise something. I hadn't noticed it before, but he must have been holding one of those spears all along. He swung it down as hard as he could upon the crystal beside him. Its tip bit into the mineral. A tiny piece flaked off, and the red light within its heart pulsed. Time slowed. I tried to sort out my legs to run, but I ended up sprawled upon the floor. Ailsa was no good. She was rooted to the spot, her mouth a perfect "O" of surprise and horror. Brett tugged the spear out of the crystal and struck it again, driving its tip in deeper. It cracked. The glow pulsed again and died. Brett yanked his spear out again, only to rain down a series of furious jabs, opening the crack wider. I scrambled to my feet and lunged for him, but he was quicker. He swung the butt of his spear up and smashed it squarely in my face. A brilliant pain erupted between my eyes, dazzling me. I stumbled back, my nose hot and heavy. Something warm trickled down my face and dripped off my chin.

"Bwett!" My whole face throbbed as I struggled to speak. "Pack it in!"

Brett ignored me. Instead, he stabbed his spear down into the crystal again, this time aiming below the crack.

"Bwett! Oh, for fug's sake..." I shook my head and wiped away the blood from my nose, trying to clear the fog. "Just stob it. Stob it, now!"

I lunged forward, and this time Brett couldn't rip the spear from the crystal in time to stop me. I used my weight to drive him backward. His face clouded over.

"What do you think you're doing?" Little flecks of spittle flew from his furious lips, and he struck out at me, again. There was no rhyme or reason to his fighting method—just a flurrying madness of fists, feet, and teeth. I defended myself as best I could, but that didn't stop him from catching me a good one on the cheek. Behind us, Ailsa screeched as the splintering groan of tortured rock filled the room. A resounding crash followed it. That was enough to stop Brett in his tracks. He leapt over me and bounded over to the crystal he had been hacking at only moments before.

A crystal that now lay in two halves.

A fluid-filled sac slithered out. Brett fell to his knees and ripped at it with both hands. Its contents, thick and stinking of brine, gushed out over him. Then, from the heart of the sac, he pulled out a soaking figure. He let out a small whimper and wrapped his arms around it. He rocked it back and forth, like a mother might soothe a fretful child, muttering something at it.

I was rooted to the spot. From the waist up, the figure

resembled a woman, albeit one with strange, mottled skin. South of her navel, though, things just went wrong. Completely wrong. That's the only way I can describe it.

Instead of legs, a writhing mass of tentacles flopped. They formed a rough ring around her hips, with thinner appendages fringing three thicker, central tentacles. The scientific part of me couldn't help but take in the details, from the way her skin took on a greenish tinge where the tentacles joined her torso to the vicious barbs hidden in their flabby suckers. I was also vaguely aware of a continuous, high pitched shrieking that echoed around the chamber, but whether it was me or Ailsa, I don't know.

Brett continued to croon at the monster, cradling her head against his shoulder, stroking her hair with a trembling hand. I couldn't understand a word he said, but Ailsa went white and stumbled over to him. She raised her hand and smacked him right across his face.

"Stop it! Just stop it! Shut up! Shut up!" There was nothing composed about her now. "Stop saying that!"

Brett, his attention still on the creature who may or may not have once been his sister, smiled.

"I have to. I have to wake her. I have to make sure it is done properly."

"No, you don't!" Ailsa's voice held a high, hysterical note. "You don't! Just leave this...this...*thing*!"

"She is not a thing!" Brett roared. "This is Marissa, my sister..." He smiled again and continued his crooning.

"No, it isn't. Can't you see? Look at it, Brett! It's...it's...it's a monster. Don't you realize? Look at it! It's not even human!"

"That's where you're wrong. They were all human once. All of them. Every single last one. They've been trapped here. Trapped, so He can use them. He called them, on the Lost Day, gathered them, those who live outside time, to show them their true purpose. From water we are, and to water they returned...to Him. To Father Dagon..."

Father Dagon? What the hell was he talking about? I stared at him in disbelief as he continued to croon at the blasphemy in his arms. Ailsa was a statue once again. I found myself able to move once more and took a faltering step toward her.

"Maybe, we should just leave—"

"And go where?" Ailsa whispered, her eyes fixated upon Brett. "Look."

I glanced down, unwilling to give Brett any more of my time. It was clear he was beyond help. I knew we now had to focus of getting out of here, but all thoughts of escape fled at the scene that was unfolding at my feet.

I thought I had seen it all. I thought there was nothing left. Nothing short of a full-on massacre could affect me, now...but I was wrong. So very wrong.

Marissa's lips were moving.

That thing was alive.

I stumbled backward.

"We...we need to get out...get away..."

"How?" Brett said, his attention still fixed on his so-called sister. "Do you really think we're still at the bottom of the ocean? On Earth?" He giggled. "You always were so close-minded, Tom. Is it so hard to believe? We aren't anywhere near Earth. We're...somewhere else. The place between the stars and reality. The place where the Great Old Ones slumber." He pointed to the glass ceiling. Another diamond had turned red. "See? The stars are finally right. The conjunction is happening. The Children of Dagon will rise, and they will prepare the way. What we discovered was merely the beginning. They started it, and the new Children will finish it. Then, They will return, and we will be nothing more than gnats upon their fantastic, celestial bodies."

As if in response to his impassioned sermon, all around us, the light from the crystals began to pulse. The torpid creatures swayed. Marissa opened her eyes and reached up to touch Brett's cheek. Brett smiled, and Marissa smiled back. He held her in his arms, tears of joy—or insanity—trickling down his face. In an unspoken agreement, Ailsa and I backed off. Some instinct deep within us both told us nothing was right with this situation. It had too much of a "happy reunion" vibe to it, and even as Marissa raised her tentacles and wrapped them around her brother is a seeming embrace, I knew what was coming next.

Ailsa buried her head into my chest as Marissa whipped her tentacles back and drove the barbs concealed within their suckers into her brother's flesh. Only then did his smile falter, replaced by a look of pitiful surprise. She stroked his hair one last time, and then squeezed, enveloping him in a mass of mottled skin. Marissa's body convulsed, further muffling his screams. Then, she flung her tentacles back, ripping chunks out of his body with them. When she finished, all that was left of Brett was a mound of mutilated meat and bone.

Marissa hauled herself up and began to drag herself across the gore-slicked ground toward us, the remains of her brother still clinging to the barbs of her tentacles.

She smiled.

"Holy shit," I hissed. As I backed away, I fumbled for Brett's spear and held it in front of me like it was some kind of magic talisman that might keep Marissa away from us. Ailsa, her tear-streaked face gaunt, snarled. From her belt, she pulled the heavy-duty spanner she had been using as a hammer.

"Bring it, bitch."

While I commended her courage, the practicality of the situation overrode any awe I felt.

"Ailsa, you can't be serious," I said. "She has about an eight-foot reach with those tentacles, and who knows what else she has up her proverbial sleeve?"

"She killed Brett."

"Yes, and she's going to kill us if we don't do something."

At the center of the circle, the rings grated, again. Above us, another diamond winked red. We had about three to go and no idea how long that would take. A strange sense of static built up around us, and the crystal pods began to vibrate. All the while, Marissa kept on smiling her vacant, oddly beatific smile as she dragged herself toward us.

I grabbed Ailsa's hand, and we ran back toward the archway. With no other options available, we skirted the edge of the dais. What had once been solid rock now rippled in a disconcerting way, and there was no way anyone could pay me to touch it, let alone run across it.

"There has to be a way to manipulate this thing," I said, running my hands over the archway, looking for anything that might give me some kind of hint as to how to operate it. "If Brett was right, these things are meant to return to Earth, which means there must be a way to activate it—force some kind of connection, or something."

"You know you sound like a total nutcase, don't you?" Ailsa asked.

I simply nodded. I was well aware of how insane I sounded. Of how insane this whole situation was, but that didn't change things. Either we found a way to open the portal, or we were mutant chow.

The crystals continued to pulse, and the torpid creatures swayed. I thought I saw movement out of the corner of my eye and whipped my head around. Marissa managed to drag herself to one of the fish-men and was busy wrapping her tentacles around it. Great. I gritted my teeth and continued my frantic search. Just was we needed—that monstrous maniac waking up her equally monstrous creators...

"Oh, come on," I implored, but the archway remained stubbornly silent.

A sharp intake of breath behind me made me pause.

"The rings!" Ailsa said. "Look at the rings!"

"What the—"

"I know. It's weird. Look at the rings. They have marks on them...some kind of writing, I think."

Aware that Marissa could tire of her current meal and drag herself down the amphitheatre steps to flay us alive at any moment, I wasn't too keen on wasting time studying what would probably turn out to be something I hadn't the hope of ever understanding. That wasn't what worried me, though.

The rings now floated about an inch above the floor. I couldn't believe Ailsa hadn't noticed.

"Ailsa...get away from that."

"There might be something here, something we could use. A code, or...or...coordinates or something."

"That may be the case, but you still need to get away." One ring moved again, but this time, there was no grating sound as it glided into place. Ailsa started back, surprised.

"They've moved."

"Yes, I can see that."

"There's something there, at the center..."

"Ailsa!"

I pulled her back before she could touch the rings.

"Hey!"

"They're all doing it. Look."

The rings were now revolving inside each other, forming what looked like a spiral that funneled down into a liquidized floor. From the inky depths of—whatever it was, now—a huge, black pillar rose. It glistened in the eerie glow of the crystals.

A hissing laugh spat from behind us. Marissa slouched mere yards away, watching us with twisted amusement.

"Father Dagon," she said, coiling her tentacles around herself. "He is called. He is here. The time is nigh!"

Ailsa and I leapt back, careful to keep the rings between us and Marissa. Between us, the pillar also continued to rise.

"No escape," Marissa said. "Just sacrifice…"

No escape. At first, I believed her. Until a glint of metal caught my eye.

Ailsa's spanner.

One way or another, we were dead, but I was damned if I was going down as a sacrifice. I wrenched it from her hand and brought it down upon one of the rings. It struck with a sound like the ringing of an enormous bell, and a visible shockwave emanated out from it. The crystals shivered, and the torpid statues jerked.

Marissa's eyes widened, and for the first time, I think I might have seen fear there.

Destroy the rings to destroy whatever gateway they were trying to summon. It seemed easy when you thought about it. I struck the ring, again. This time, a bolt of electricity shot up my arm, making me squawk and my heart to run ragged in my chest. The ring wobbled, causing it to oscillate on its own axis, like a dropped plate. Marissa screeched.

"Stop it! Stop it! You don't know what you are doing!"

She lay flat on the ground and commenced dragging herself around the spiral toward us. She didn't dare fling her tentacles at us, not across the rings.

Ailsa caught on quickly. I had her spanner, so all she had left was her flashlight. She smashed it down upon the ring. The glass smashed, and she hissed as a fragment caught her on her hand. Blood flowed. A drop spilled from her fingertips, onto the ring.

From the center of the now-crooked spiral , a guttural roar rang out. It wasn't unlike the sound that had knocked us out in the sub. Around us, every single crystal exploded. We fell to the ground as lethal shards spun through the air, slashing into the waking guardians, felling most of them before they were fully awake. Those who escaped death croaked their bewilderment and tore into the slippery sacks at their feet, hoping to find their acolytes but instead found bags of mangled flesh.

Marissa moaned and covered her head with her hands as a particularly huge chunk of crystal smashed down onto the rings, ripping one completely from its moorings and sending it spinning toward her. Its momentum didn't slow as it sliced her head clean from her shoulders.

The head bumped down into the spiral, and the archway fizzed and blinked, its surface winking in and out of reality.

I had no idea what lay on the other side, but whatever it was, it had to be better than what was here. All around us, the fish creatures were waking up, running around, helping the surviving mutants out of what remained of their crystals. Some of them looked like Marissa, as half humans, but others were true nightmares—fusions of deep-sea creatures and other, even more alien monsters.

The archway continued to blink, like a television trying to find a channel. I grabbed Ailsa's hand. The Children of Dagon gathered around us and the fractal remains of the spiral. A vile, sulfurous stench arose from it, and a column of something black and oily erupted upward to consume the pillar just as the last diamond blinked crimson.

The stars, it would seem, were finally right, but everything else wasn't. The black column fought to maintain its integrity, twisting itself into a myriad of forms but finding none. The Children of Dagon, caught between ecstasy and terror, wailed. I dragged Ailsa around the edge of the column and toward the archway. It still couldn't establish a stable portal but continued to flicker in and out of existence.

The column swelled. Around it, the rings began to crack. The Children of Dagon howled.

The portal blinked on, and Ailsa and I jumped.

Chapter Ten

What happened after that? I'm not entirely sure. I'm not even sure where we are. I think it's somewhere on Earth, but I could be wrong. I think the stars look right, but I never was much of an astronomer. I always preferred the ocean and spent most of my life looking down rather than up.

The fish we catch are strange. I kind of recognize their genus, but their species eludes me. Luckily, they are edible.

The archway opened up onto an island. The whole structure was vibrating by the time we popped out. We barely had time to clear the surface before there was this weird kind of implosion that took out the archway completely. There's literally nothing left of it.

Our only hope of leaving this place is now by rescue. We've been here a couple of nights, and it's been pretty peaceful. All I can hear is the swish of the surf and the call of unseen birds. We tend to stay near the beach. Ailsa won't go near the water, though. We've made a fire and keep it going at all times. Hopefully, someone will fly over us or a boat will pass nearby, and they'll see our smoke signal. That's if there is anyone out there to rescue us, of course. I haven't spoken to Ailsa about this, but I am wondering. There hasn't been any evidence whatsoever of human interference on the island, which worries me. Even uninhabited islands have rubbish wash up on their beaches, but this one has nothing. I can't help but wonder if we're even on Earth, sometimes. Who knows? We might have catapulted down the wrong thread of time, to an Earth where dinosaurs still roam.

I've decided to write down everything that happened to us in my notebook. That's the good thing about being a scientist. You don't go anywhere without a notebook. I'm hoping it will help me come to terms with everything.

I don't know what Ailsa is going to do. She spends most of her time just sitting, staring into the fire. She eats when I give her things to eat, drinks when I give her water to drink, but that's it. Like I said, she won't go near the sea. She won't even look at it. Me? I can't take my eyes off it. Who knows what's out there, waiting in the depths. I for one won't be caught off guard. Not again.

Ailsa hardly speaks. When she does, all she says is she can hear drums. Drums that pound with a steady rhythm. I can't hear them. At least, that's what I tell myself.

After all...who knows?

Right?

About the Author:

CJ Waller lives in the UK with her husband, daughters, cats and various dinosaurs. She spends her days writing about alternate dimensions and mad gods and drawing inappropriately dressed fantasy figures, waiting for a time when the stars are finally right.

Visit her website:
http://adarkwhimsy.wordpress.com/
Twitter: @ADarkWhimsy

Also from Damnation Books:

Sharkways
by A.J. Kirby

eBook ISBN: 9781615727728
Print ISBN: 9781615727735

Horror Monster
Novella of 53,271 words

Bill Minto is a world-weary property developer. His marriage is on the rocks. His health is failing. His cut-cornered projects constantly threaten to come back and haunt him.

When a mysterious caller offers him the job of a lifetime—all he must do is excavate the hidden tunnels under a country house—he jumps at the chance.

It becomes clear Bill is not alone in the tunnels. A past he long believed hidden lurches after him in the darkness, smelling blood. And guilt.

Also from Damnation Books:

Jars in the Cellar
by Lee Clark Zumpe

eBook ISBN: 9781615720477

Lovecraftian Horror
Short Story of 6,125 words

Welcome to Hadoth Creek; population: dwindling. An unscheduled detour reroutes Henry Bickleworth from his intended itinerary, transporting him to this peculiar, secluded enclave which clings to tradition and an unconventional past. Sheltered and isolated from the modern world, Hadoth Creek harbors unsettling secrets and ancient horrors—as Henry Bickleworth soon discovers.

Visit Damnation Books online at:

Our Blog—
http://www.damnationbooks.com/blog/

DB Reader's Yahoogroup—
http://groups.yahoo.com/group/DamnationBooks/

Twitter—
http://twitter.com/DamnationBooks

Google+—
https://plus.google.com/u/0/115524941844122973800

Facebook—
https://www.facebook.com/pages/
Damnation-Books/80339241586

Goodreads—
http://www.goodreads.com/DamnationBooks

Shelfari—
http://www.shelfari.com/damnationbooks

Library Thing—
http://www.librarything.com/DamnationBooks

HorrorWorld Forums—
http://horrorworld.org/phpBB3/viewforum.php?f=134

Printed by BoD™ in Norderstedt, Germany